MOTORSPORTS ENCYCLOPEDIAS

THE FORMULA 1 ENCYCLOPEDIA

BY PRIYANKA LAMICHHANE

Encyclopedias

An Imprint of Abdo Reference

abdobooks.com

TABLE OF CONTENTS

ORACLE
HONDA
Red Bull
ROKT
Esso
Claro
aws

HISTORY OF FORMULA 1

Formula 1 is one of the most exciting motorsports in the world. Its roots can be traced back to early car racing in Europe during the late 19th century.

Car racing began soon after the invention of gas-powered automobiles in the late 1880s. At that time, racing was happening in different parts of Europe, especially within and around France. The first official car race took place in 1895. The round-trip race was from Paris to Bordeaux, a distance of 732 miles (1,178 km). At that time, cars were not as fast as they are today. The average speed during this race was just 15 miles per hour (24 kmh).

These early races were happening on the open road, and there were no rules or safety regulations. By 1904, the Fédération Internationale de l'Automobile was established to

Course de Périgueux, the first closed-circuit racecourse

FORMULA 1: F.Y.I.

In 1898, the first closed-circuit racecourse was built in southwest France. Closed-circuit means that the track is enclosed and not part of the open road.

1908 race car

help organize drivers and races. It also began to create safety standards. *Fédération Internationale de l'Automobile* means "International Automobile Federation" in English. It is often called "FIA."

FUN FACT

The "Formula" in Formula 1 refers to the set of rules that drivers and teams must follow.

Open-wheel racing was all the rage by 1931. Open-wheel cars have their wheels outside the body of the car instead of underneath. During this time, there was an attempt to organize open-wheel races, but the effort was put on hold when World War II began in 1939. It wasn't until after the war in 1946 that the FIA set forth rules for open-wheel racing and for a championship race. These races became known as Formula 1. Formula 1 is sometimes shortened to "F1."

FORMULA 1'S FIRST RACE

The first Formula 1 race took place in 1950 in Silverstone, England. This was around the same time NASCAR began in the United States. The race was known as the British Grand Prix and was the first of seven races in Formula 1's first season.

The race took place with The United Kingdom's King George VI, his wife Queen Consort Elizabeth, and their daughter Princess Margaret in attendance. Participants drove on an airfield

FUN FACT

Prince Bira from Thailand was one of the drivers in the first Formula 1 race.

Guiseppe Farina races at the first Formula 1 race.

that had been used during World War II. The cars raced on the paved runway. More than 100,000 people came to watch.

The race consisted of a total of 70 laps and lasted just over two hours. The winner was Giuseppe Farina of Italy. His car was an Italian-made vehicle called the Alfa Romeo. The powerful car won the majority of races it competed in at the time. Giuseppe's two Italian teammates, who also drove Alfa Romeos, came in second and third place.

Racing drivers Alberto Ascari, Juan Manuel Fangio, and Giuseppe Farina at Silverstone

FORMULA 1: F.Y.I.

Formula 1 races are also known as a *Grand Prix, which* means "grand prize" in French. The first known use of this term in racing was for the Grand Prix de Paris, a horse race that began in 1863.

1937 Alfa Romeo

FORMULA 1: WORLD'S MOST POPULAR RACES

The first time Formula 1 was on television was in 1953, but at that time, only parts of a race were aired. It was not until the early 1980s that entire races, from start to finish, were shown on television. Today, Formula 1 has a huge global audience. In 2022, each Formula 1 race had more than 1.2 million viewers in the United States alone. The races get more than 440 million viewers around the world, and attendance at the races is also very high. In 2022, almost 6 million people went to see a Formula 1 race.

There are a few reasons why Formula 1 is so popular. First, it has international appeal. The races take place all over the world, from the United States to Japan and everywhere in between. Formula 1 has also taken advantage of engaging fans through social media and global television broadcasting. In

Fans celebrate at the Italian Grand Prix.

Alberto Ascari leads in the 1953 French Grand Prix.

addition, Formula 1 racing pushes the boundaries of technology with carmakers building some of the most advanced cars in auto racing.

FORMULA 1: F.Y.I.

The 1995 Australian Grand Prix holds the record for the best-attended Formula race weekend of all time. There were 520,000 fans who enjoyed the events.

1995 Australian Grand Prix

TIMELINE

1901
The term "grand prix" was used for the first time to describe a car race.

1906
The first official Grand Prix race was held in France.

1900s | 1910s | 1920s | 1930s | 1940s | 1950s

1904
The International Automobile Federation, FIA, was established.

1950
The first Formula 1 World Championship race was held in Silverstone, England.

1930s
Plans were made for the first Formula 1 race. The race was put on hold because of the start of World War II.

1975

Maria Grazia "Lella" Lombardi became the first woman to score points in Formula 1.

2007

Lewis Hamilton became the first Black Formula 1 driver.

1960s | 1970s | 1980s | 1990s | 2000s | 2010s

1970S

Race cars became faster and more powerful. The first turbocharged cars were used.

2019

The 1,000th Grand Prix was held in Shanghai, China.

1990

The 500th Grand Prix took place in Adelaide, Australia.

DIAGRAM OF A FORMULA 1 CAR

The FIA regulates every detail of all of the cars on the tracks. These details include the length and weight of the cars as well as the type of engine they use. The car regulations together are known as the car's "formula."

Consistency among all the cars is very important. It ensures that all drivers and teams are on a fair playing field.

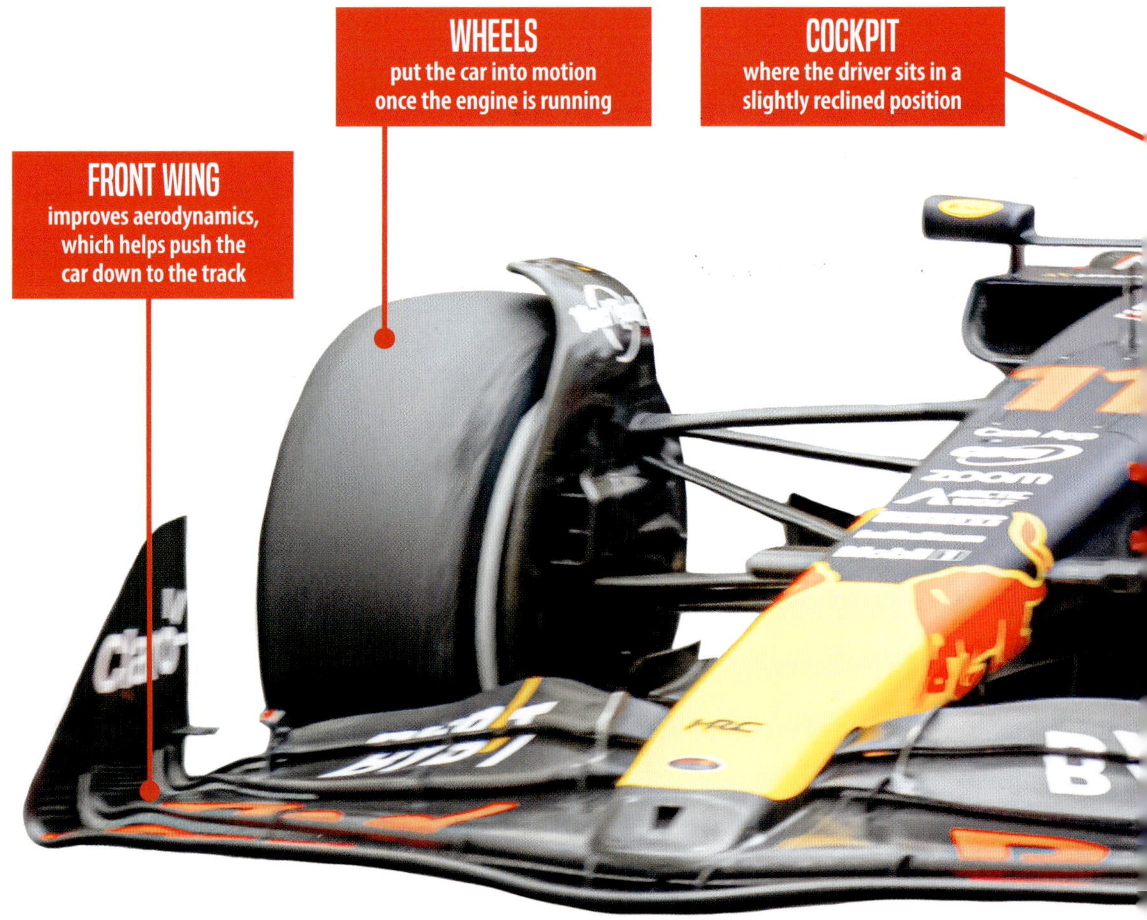

FUN FACT

Formula 1 cars can reach speeds of over 200 miles per hour (322 kmh).

BUILDING A FORMULA 1 CAR

A Formula 1 car is a complex machine made up of 14,500 different parts. Each Formula 1 team builds a new car for each racing season. The process starts right after the current year's car is unveiled, and it takes about one year.

First, drivers provide the teams' engineers with feedback on the current cars: what has gone well and what can be improved. Designers then create sketches and computer images for new design concepts. Within the larger design group, there are smaller groups that specialize in transmission, electronics, mechanics, and aerodynamics. All designers have to follow the rules set by the FIA when developing their concepts.

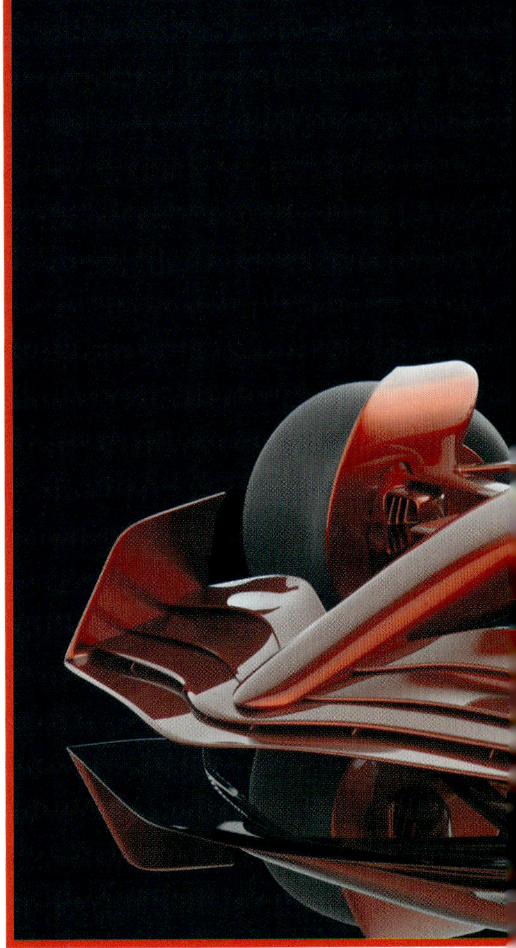

FORMULA 1: F.Y.I.

Formula 1 is made up of 10 racing teams. Each F1 team can have up to four drivers, but only two can drive in a race. The teams build their own cars based on the rules set out by the FIA. Drivers on the same team drive the same model car, but each driver can choose to make some adjustments within the rules.

From there, the best design moves forward to the building stage. The car is built at 60 percent of its full size. Engineers then test the model for important design elements such as aerodynamics.

FUN FACT

In 2023, a Formula 1 car cost almost $16 million to build.

Once the building team is happy with the design, the car is manufactured. It is built with carbon fiber, a light yet strong material. Every piece of the car is carefully put together. Even the glue that's used has to be exactly the right color so it does not take away from the color of the car.

FOR THE FANS! A GRAND PRIX WEEKEND

A Formula 1 Grand Prix takes place over a few days, usually starting on a Thursday, and there is much for fans to do. First, fans are treated to a pit lane walk where they get a close-up look at cars and drivers as they prepare for the race. Friday features two practice sessions that are open for fans to watch. Each practice is 90 minutes long.

Drivers take part in a qualifying race on Saturday, the day before the main race. The qualifying race is divided into three sessions, and the goal is to determine the starting positions for the main race. The slowest drivers are eliminated in sessions one and two, leaving the top 10 fastest drivers. These drivers race in the third session of the qualifier. The winner of this session gets to start in the pole position, which is the first spot on the inside front row. This position gives a driver a starting advantage because it is ahead of all the other drivers. That makes three races that fans get to watch before the main race even begins.

Fans enjoy a pit lane walk at the Hungarian Grand Prix.

Race winners each get a trophy at the podium.

Sunday is the big day—it's time for the main race, which begins at 2:00 in the afternoon. The race can last from one and a half to two hours. Once the race ends, the top three drivers stand on a podium in their respective spots. Fans get to go out onto the track to watch the winners' ceremony.

FORMULA 1: F.Y.I.

Some Formula 1 drivers have their own traditions after winning a race. One of the most interesting comes from Australian driver Daniel Ricciardo. If he makes it onto the podium in first, second, or third place, he drinks champagne from one of his racing shoes.

Daniel Ricciardo's tradition is called a "shoey."

START YOUR ENGINES!

Formula 1 holds races in numerous countries across five different continents. These races are the highest level of car racing competition in the world. A Formula 1 season is made up of a series of 21 to 24 races known as a Grand Prix. The season starts in March and ends in December. Some races are held on circuits, which are tracks designed just for racing. Others are held on roads that are closed for the race.

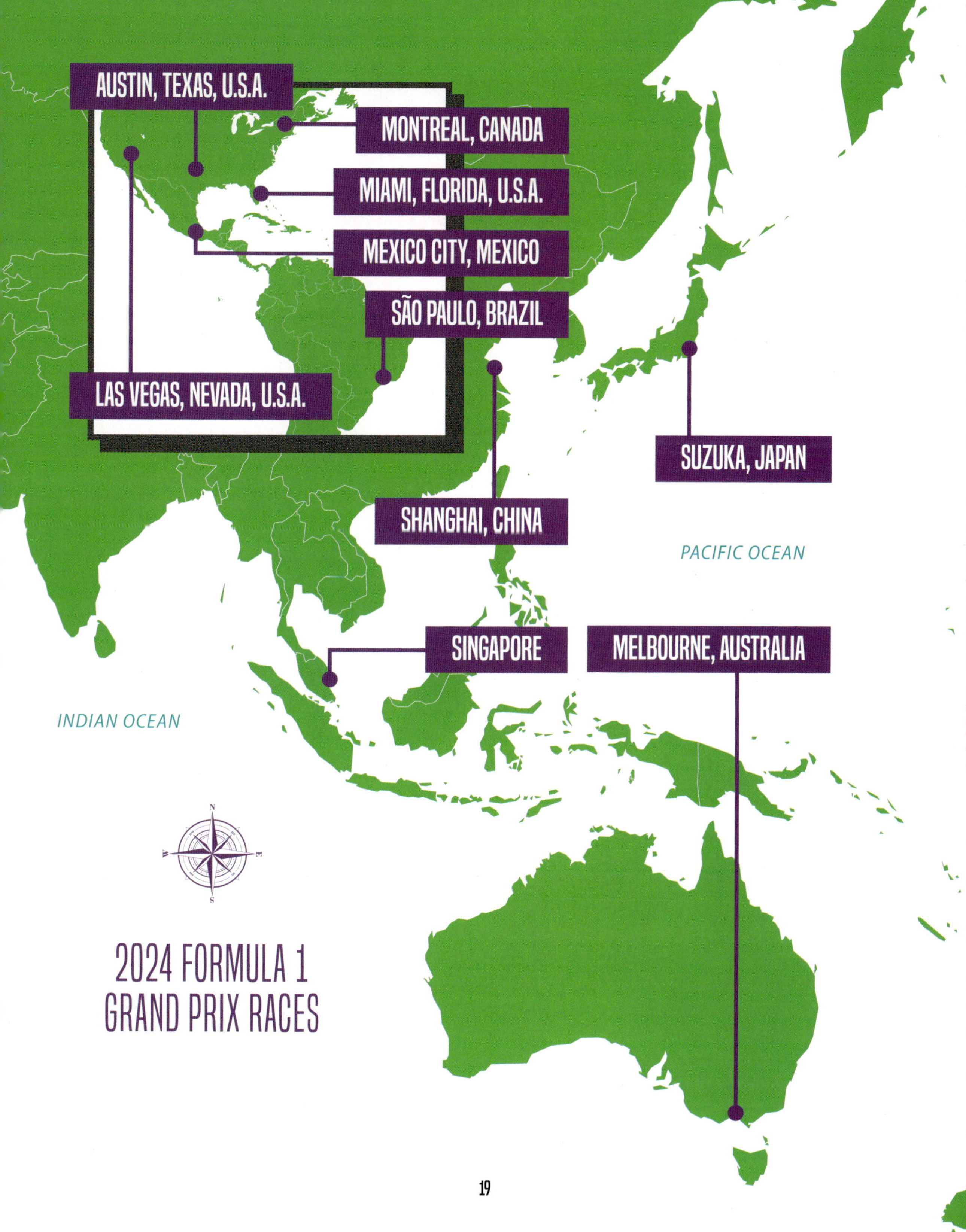
AUSTIN, TEXAS, U.S.A.
MONTREAL, CANADA
MIAMI, FLORIDA, U.S.A.
MEXICO CITY, MEXICO
SÃO PAULO, BRAZIL
LAS VEGAS, NEVADA, U.S.A.
SUZUKA, JAPAN
SHANGHAI, CHINA
PACIFIC OCEAN
SINGAPORE
MELBOURNE, AUSTRALIA
INDIAN OCEAN
N
E
S
W
2024 FORMULA 1
GRAND PRIX RACES

ABU DHABI GRAND PRIX

The Abu Dhabi Grand Prix started in 2009. It takes place at the Yas Marina Circuit in Abu Dhabi, United Arab Emirates. It was the first F1 race named after the host city instead of the host country. Today, Mexico City, São Paulo, and Miami have been added to that list.

The Yas Marina Circuit usually holds the very last race of the season. The track is designed

FUN FACT

The Yas Marina Circuit track passes underneath the W Abu Dhabi Hotel where rooms have a direct view of the track.

Sergio Perez competes for Red Bull Racing at the Abu Dhabi Grand Prix.

to change into six different configurations, depending on what racing series is taking place. The event as a whole is well-known for its flashy nighttime light display.

What's unique about this raceway is that it's on an island next to a marina. Yas Marina Circuit shares the island with the Yas Waterworld waterpark and Ferrari World theme park, home to the world's fastest rollercoaster.

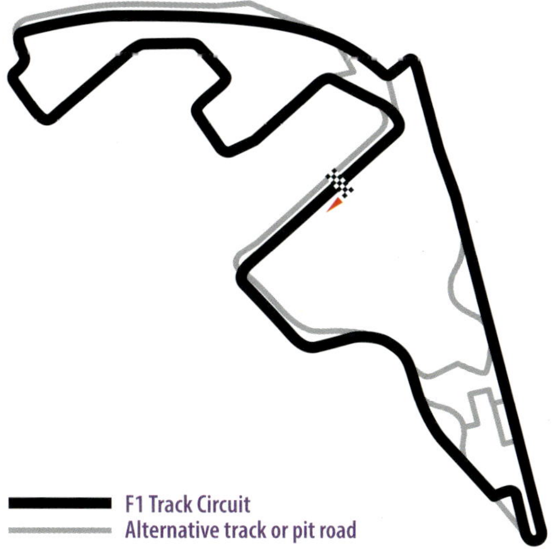

TRACK STATS

- **Year opened**: 2009
- **Length**: 3.3 miles (5 km)
- **Number of laps in the race**: 58
- **Number of turns**: 16

AUSTRALIAN GRAND PRIX

The Australian Grand Prix in Melbourne, Australia, takes place at the Albert Park Circuit, a street circuit that surrounds Albert Park Lake.

The majority of the Albert Park Circuit is made up of public roads, which are closed during the race. About two months before the Grand Prix begins, structures, such as fencing, the grandstand, and overpasses, are assembled.

Though this track in its current configuration was opened in 1996, the original track was built in the 1950s. The first Grand Prix race was

FUN FACT

An area of the neighboring sea was separated off to create the estuary around Albert Park Circuit.

Fans can enjoy views of the scenic Albert Park Lake while watching the action of the Australian Grand Prix.

held there in 1953, but five years later, the track was closed. The local government didn't want the track in their area. The track wasn't used for about 30 years, but in 1992, Melbourne's government wanted to draw more people to the city. After about four years of preparation, the track reopened in 1996.

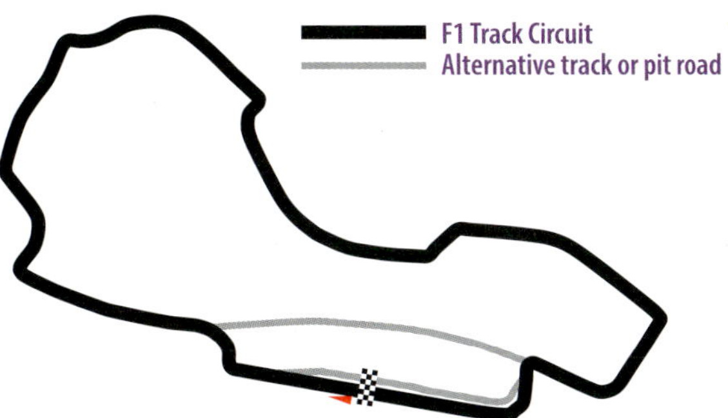

TRACK STATS

- **Year opened**: 1996
- **Length**: 3.3 miles (5 km)
- **Number of laps in the race**: 58
- **Number of turns:** 14

Daniel Ricciardo drives the number 3 McLaren at the Australian Grand Prix.

AUSTRIAN GRAND PRIX

The Austrian Grand Prix is held at the Red Bull Ring in Spielberg, Austria. The track has been around since the 1960s. It is known for its stunning mountain backdrop. It has been in its current state since 2011, but before that, the track went through many changes.

In 1963, the track was an air base. The paved road of the air base was bumpy and hard to drive on, and

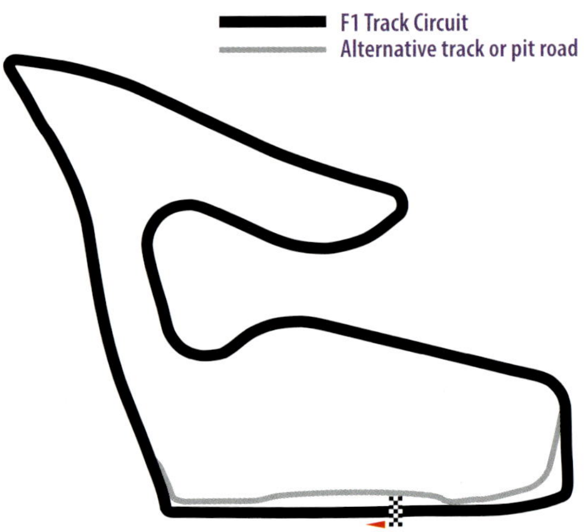

TRACK STATS

- **Year opened**: 2011
- **Length**: 2.7 miles (4 km)
- **Number of laps in the race**: 71
- **Number of turns**: 10

FUN FACT

The Red Bull Ring has a huge steel statue of a bull, right in the middle of the track. It stands at 56 feet (17 m).

Aerial view of the Red Bull Ring

drivers didn't like it. By 1969, the air base had been rebuilt into the Österreichring racetrack. The track's first race was 621 miles (1,000 km) around. The following year, the Österreichring held its first Grand Prix. More than 100,000 fans showed up to watch the excitement.

The Österreichring track later became the A1 Ring, with a brand-new layout. It remained this way through the 1990s and early 2000s. In 2011, the track was reopened as the new and upgraded Red Bull Ring.

AZERBAIJAN GRAND PRIX

The Azerbaijan Grand Prix is a race held on the Baku City Circuit in Baku, Azerbaijan. It is the fourth-longest racetrack in Formula 1 and sits right in the middle of a city. However, the first Grand Prix held in the city was the European Grand Prix in 2016. It was the country's way of showing that they too could hold F1 races that would attract legions of fans.

The first city track required more than 1,500 concrete blocks

FUN FACT

Azerbaijan is known as the land of fire. It is home to a naturally burning fire known as Yanar Dağ. The fire has been burning for more than 65 years.

Max Verstappen races past historic buildings during the Azerbaijan Grand Prix.

F1 drivers race on the streets of Baku, Azerbaijan.

to be placed along the streets to serve as safety barriers. After the streets were prepared, the race was held. It proved to be a huge success, but it caused major traffic jams. Due to the traffic issues, the race moved to a new location in the city.

Today's Baku City Circuit, which officially started holding races in 2017, winds through the historic city center, and fans get to see a blend of modern racing and old architecture. The circuit has very narrow areas and straight-line areas known as "high-speed straights," both of which make for action-packed races.

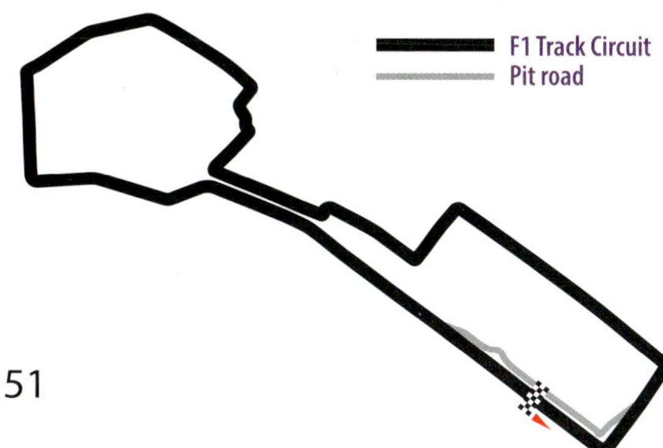

TRACK STATS

- **Year opened**: 2016
- **Length**: 3.7 miles (6 km)
- **Number of laps in the race**: 51
- **Number of turns**: 20

BAHRAIN GRAND PRIX

The Bahrain Grand Prix is one of the most popular Formula 1 races. It is held at the Bahrain International Circuit in Sakhir, Bahrain. It was the first Formula 1 race in the Middle East. What makes this track unique is its setting: the track sits in the middle of the Sakhir Desert.

The Bahrain International Circuit can be reconfigured

TRACK STATS

- **Year opened**: 2004
- **Length**: 3.4 miles (5 km)
- **Number of laps in the race**: 57
- **Number of turns**: 15

F1 Track Circuit
Alternative track or pit road

Prior to each race, a sticky substance is sprayed on the surrounding desert to keep sand off the track.

A Ferrari logo is displayed on a building during the Bahrain Grand Prix.

into five different layouts depending on the racing event. There are long straights and difficult corners along the track, and at night, the raceway is brightly lit, giving fans a unique nighttime race experience.

FUN FACT

It took 496 days to complete the construction of the Bahrain International Circuit—that's less than 1.5 years.

BELGIAN GRAND PRIX

The Belgian Grand Prix takes place at the Circuit de Spa-Francorchamps, located in the Ardennes Forest of Belgium. Circuit de Spa-Francorchamps first opened soon after World War I. Car races had been happening in Belgium and around Europe, but the war put a stop to the events for a number of years. After the track was established, it became a popular place for car and

FUN FACT

The Circuit de Spa-Francorchamps first opened more than 100 years ago. The original circuit was 9.8 miles (16 km) around, much longer than it is today.

The Eau Rouge corner is considered one of the most difficult corners in all of Formula 1.

Charles Leclerc races a Ferrari at the Belgian Grand Prix.

motorbike racing until the start of World War II in 1939. Again, the track closed, but it was reopened seven years later, in 1946. By 1950, the first Belgium Grand Prix for Formula 1 was held, and the races have continued at the track ever since.

This track is known for its unpredictable weather—it rains a lot. The track is also known for the Eau Rouge corner, a section that is a steep uphill drive. *Eau Rouge* means "red water" in French.

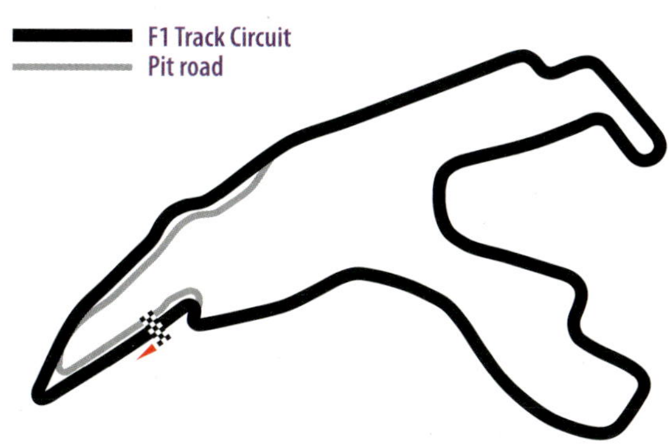

TRACK STATS

- **Year opened**: 1921
- **Length**: 4.4 miles (7 km)
- **Number of laps in the race**: 44
- **Number of turns**: 19

BRITISH GRAND PRIX

The Silverstone Circuit in Silverstone, England, is home to the British Grand Prix. Silverstone is one of the oldest F1 tracks in the world.

The track was once an airfield used during World War II. After the war, the Royal Automobile Club started using the airfield for car races. The first was the British Grand Prix in 1950. This was also the first Formula 1 Grand Prix as well as the first World Championship round.

In the early 1990s, the track went through major renovations for

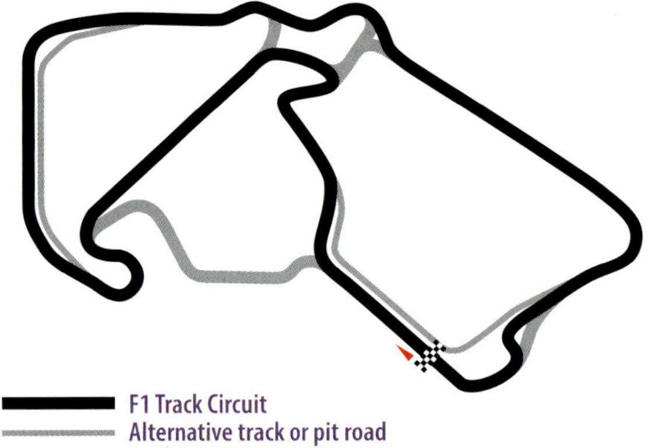

TRACK STATS

- **Year opened**: 1948
- **Length**: 3.7 miles (6 km)
- **Number of laps in the race**: 52
- **Number of turns**: 18

Pierre Gasly competes for Alpine at the British Grand Prix.

Fans look on as Carlos Sainz Jr. races at the Silverstone Circuit.

general updates and to improve driver safety. Today, the Silverstone Circuit is known for its high-speed corners, including the Copse, one of the fastest corners in F1 racing.

FUN FACT

The British Grand Prix at the Silverstone Circuit is one of the most popular races in the world. In 2023, 480,000 fans were in attendance. Only one other race, the 1995 Australian Grand Prix, had a higher attendance.

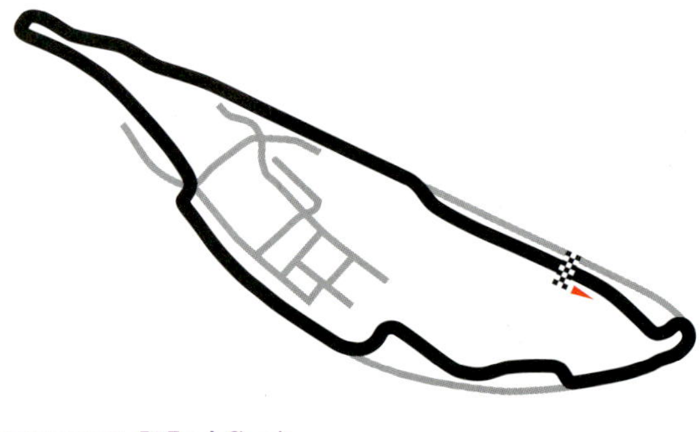

F1 Track Circuit
Alternative track, service road, or pit road

CANADIAN GRAND PRIX

The Canadian Grand Prix takes place on an island in the heart of the Saint Lawrence River. The track, called the Circuit Gilles Villeneuve, is located on Notre Dame Island in Montreal, Canada. It is surrounded by greenery and outdoor artwork, making for a scenic view all along the raceway.

The track itself is a challenging one, with sharp bends and tight turns, making it perfect for action-packed races. In 1982, the track was renamed from the

TRACK STATS

- **Year opened**: 1978
- **Length**: 2.7 miles (4 km)
- **Number of laps in the race**: 70
- **Number of turns**: 14

FUN FACT

The St. Lawrence River connects the Great Lakes to the Atlantic Ocean. Together, the Great Lakes make up the largest freshwater system in the world.

Lance Stroll drives for Aston Martin at the Canadian Grand Prix.

Circuit Gilles Villeneuve, located on Notre Dame Island

Ile Notre-Dame Circuit to the Circuit Gilles Villeneuve Circuit to honor Gilles Villeneuve, a famous Canadian Formula 1 driver from Montreal. He won the track's first-ever F1 race in 1978.

When not hosting the Canadian Grand Prix, the Circuit Gilles Villeneuve Circuit is open for local residents to use for walking, running, skating, and other outdoor activities.

CHINESE GRAND PRIX

The Chinese Grand Prix takes place at the Shanghai International Circuit. Construction on the track began in 2003, and the first Chinese Grand Prix was held in 2004.

The track was designed to look like the Chinese symbol for *shang*, which means "upwards." With this design come several unique hairpins and S-shaped turns. Many spectators find that

Lewis Hamilton leads at the 2019 Chinese Grand Prix.

Spectators watch as cars race through the turns at the Shanghai International Circuit.

the hairpin at turns 14 and 15 (at the lower left) is the best place to watch a race. It is a section of the track known for overtaking.

Due to COVID-19, the Chinese Grand Prix was absent from the Formula 1 line-up for four seasons, from 2020 to 2023. The Chinese Grand Prix returned to Formula 1 in 2024.

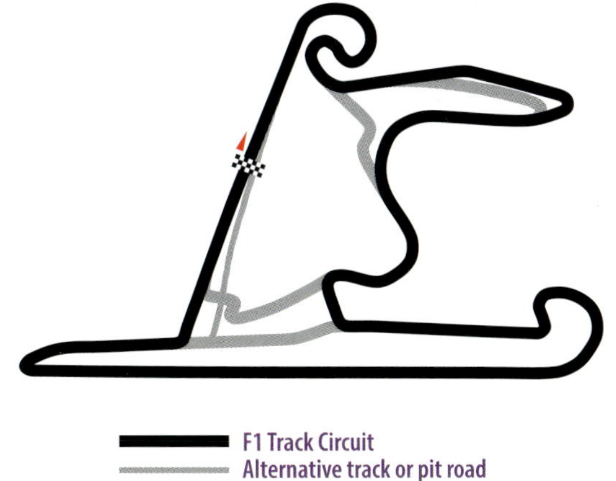

TRACK STATS

- **Year opened**: 2004
- **Length**: 3.9 miles (6 km)
- **Number of laps in the race**: 56
- **Number of turns**: 16

DUTCH GRAND PRIX

The Dutch Grand Prix takes place on a historic track, the Zandvoort Circuit in Zandvoort, Netherlands. The Zandvoort Circuit has a long history, dating back to the 1930s. In 1939, before the track was built, the first official car race in Zandvoort was organized by local car racing enthusiasts. Though there was no track, it turned out to be a big success. This race opened the doors to making Zandvoort a popular car racing destination.

Zandvoort Circuit

Max Verstappen leads at the Dutch Grand Prix.

Plans were laid to build a racetrack, but due to World War II, construction was delayed. The track, first named Circuit Park Zandvoort, eventually opened in 1948. It held its first Formula 1 race, the Dutch Grand Prix, in 1952.

The Zandvoort Circuit is located among sand dunes, which makes it both special and challenging. The track has banked, or high, corners and fast straights. In addition, a campsite is located next to the track, allowing spectators to experience races close-up.

TRACK STATS

- **Year opened**: 1948
- **Length**: 2.6 miles (4 km)
- **Number of laps in the race**: 72
- **Number of turns**: 14

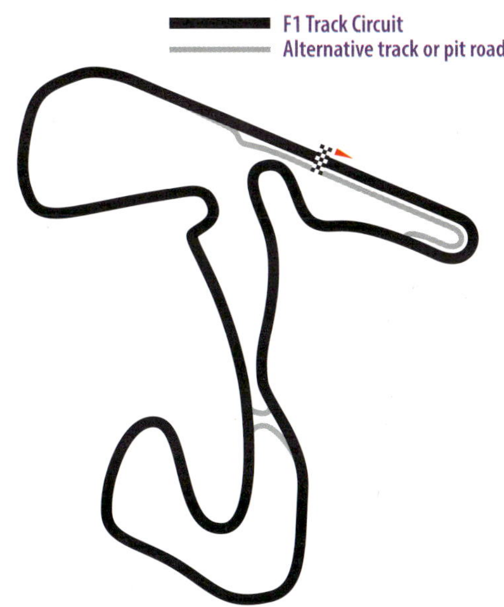

FUN FACT

The Zandvoort Circuit is located close to the sea, providing a scenic backdrop for racing events.

F1 Track Circuit
Alternative track or pit road

EMILIA-ROMAGNA GRAND PRIX

The Emilia-Romagna Grand Prix takes place in the city of Imola, Italy. But cars were not the first vehicles to run on this track. Motorcycle races began here in the early 1950s. The first layout of the track was a connection of the city's roads. It wasn't until the 1970s that a permanent track was created. The first F1 race was held in the early

TRACK STATS

- **Year opened**: 1953
- **Length**: 3.1 miles (5 km)
- **Number of laps in the race**: 63
- **Number of turns**: 19

Sparks fly during the Emilia-Romagna Grand Prix.

The town's name of Imola is painted on the track.

1980s, under the name San Marino Grand Prix, but the name was changed to Emilia-Romagna in 2020.

During the 2023 F1 season, the Emilia-Romagna Grand Prix was canceled due to heavy flooding in the area. Luckily, the track wasn't badly damaged and the race was back on for 2024. With its many sharp turns, the Emilia-Romagna is known as one of the most difficult circuits in Europe.

A memorial for Ayrton Senna was built after his death during the Emilia-Romagna Grand Prix.

HUNGARIAN GRAND PRIX

The Hungarian Grand Prix was the first Formula 1 race held in Eastern Europe. The track is located at the Hungaroring Circuit in Mogyoród, Hungary. It is known for its tight and twisty layout, which makes it challenging for drivers to overtake each other during a race.

Prior to World War II, car racing was a popular sport in Hungary. But official car racing was put on hold during the war. After the war, much of Europe, including Hungary, was focused on rebuilding. Car racing was not a priority.

Race cars take off at the start of the Hungarian Grand Prix.

Hungaroring Circuit

But by the 1980s, Hungarians wanted to promote tourism in their country. Car racing would be a way to do so. The Hungaroring Circuit was built in a record eight months, beginning in October 1985. The following year, the first Formula 1 Hungarian Grand Prix race took place with an audience of 200,000.

TRACK STATS

- **Year opened**: 1986
- **Length**: 2.7 miles (4 km)
- **Number of laps in the race**: 70
- **Number of turns**: 14

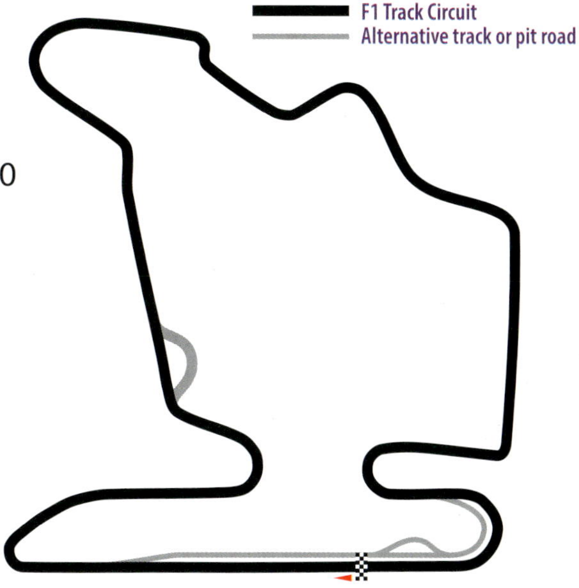

FUN FACT

The Hungaroring Circuit sits in a valley, providing spectators good views of the track from most seats.

ITALIAN GRAND PRIX

The Italian Grand Prix has been widely popular in Italy for almost 100 years. In the early 1920s, the Italian motor industry was beginning to boom. Races were one way to show off Italian cars, and interest in constructing a racetrack began to grow.

On February 26, 1922, construction workers broke ground on a new racetrack, the Monza Circuit, in Monza, which is located north of Milan, Italy. More than 3,000 workers were brought in to get the track done as fast as possible. A temporary railroad track was also built to quickly bring in construction supplies. The raceway was done in 110 days—just over three months. By the time of its completion, the Monza

TRACK STATS

- **Year opened**: 1922
- **Length**: 3.6 miles (6 km)
- **Number of laps in the race**: 53
- **Number of turns**: 11

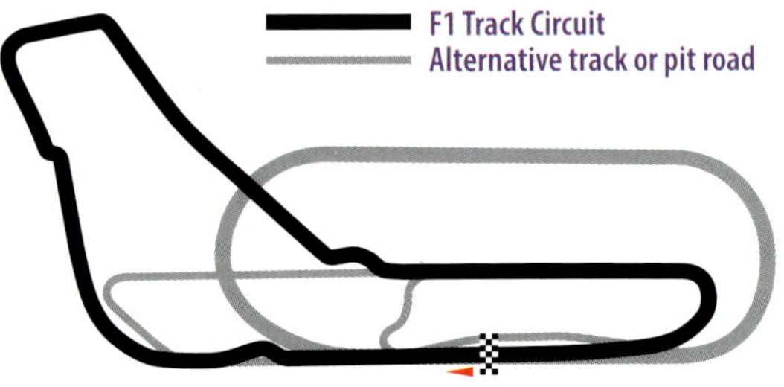

Tifosi, the supporters of Italy's Scuderia Ferrari team, are known for their lively celebrations.

Monza Circuit

Circuit was the third car racing track ever built.

Today, the Monza Circuit track is the fastest in all of Formula 1. This is in part due to its simple oval shape. Without as many tight curves as other tracks, cars can go faster.

FUN FACT

The Monza Circuit is the home to legendary teams, including Ferrari.

JAPANESE GRAND PRIX

The Suzuka International Racing Course in Suzuka, Japan, is home to the Japanese Grand Prix. The track is one of the most challenging F1 circuits in the world. The track has a unique figure eight shape, which means it has twists at the center. In addition, it has many different types of corners that

FUN FACT

The Suzuka International Racing Course is part of the Suzuka Circuit, which includes a resort and an amusement park. Spectators can see the entire racecourse from the Ferris wheel.

Ferris wheel riders look on as Lance Stroll races by on the Suzuka International Racing Course.

pose varying levels of difficulty for drivers.

In the 1960s, before the track was built, the area for the raceway was surrounded by fields of rice paddies. In 1961, John Hugenholtz, who also designed the Zandvoort Circuit in the Netherlands, began designing the Suzuka International Racing Course. The track opened in 1962 and served as a test track for Honda, which is headquartered in Japan. The track began hosting a variety of car races and motorcycle events. It held its first Formula 1 race, the Japanese Grand Prix, in 1987. Today, the venue can hold 155,000 people.

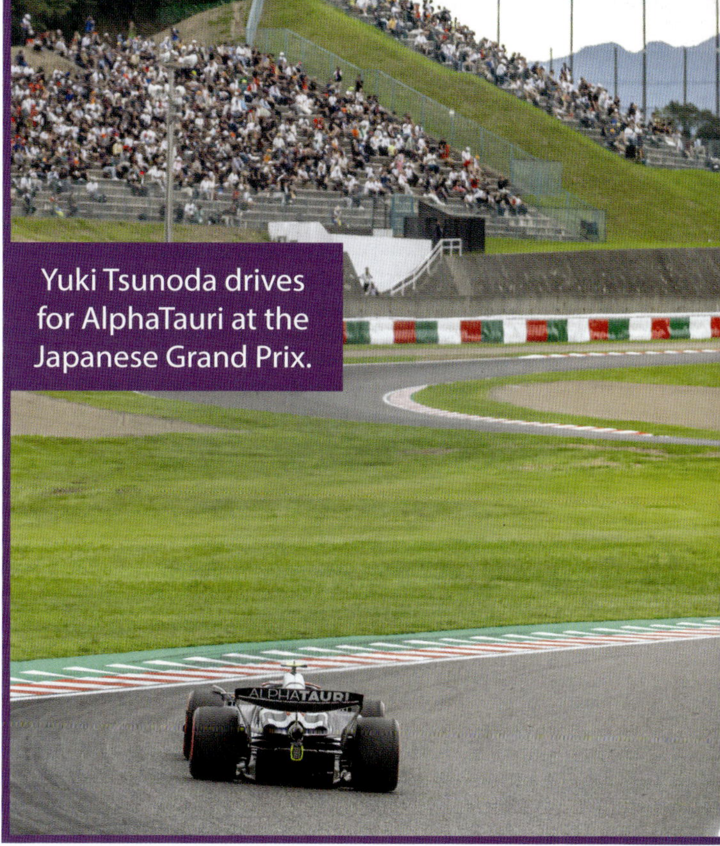

Yuki Tsunoda drives for AlphaTauri at the Japanese Grand Prix.

TRACK STATS

- **Year opened**: 1962
- **Length**: 3.6 miles (6 km)
- **Number of laps in the race**: 53
- **Number of turns**: 18

LAS VEGAS GRAND PRIX

The Las Vegas Grand Prix is held at night in the heart of Las Vegas, Nevada. The course runs along Las Vegas Boulevard, also called the Strip, one of the most famous roads in the world. The Strip is known for its casinos, hotels, and flashy displays of lights.

FUN FACT

The Las Vegas Grand Prix weaves by some of the most popular hotels on the Strip, including the Bellagio, Caesar's Palace, and Paris Las Vegas.

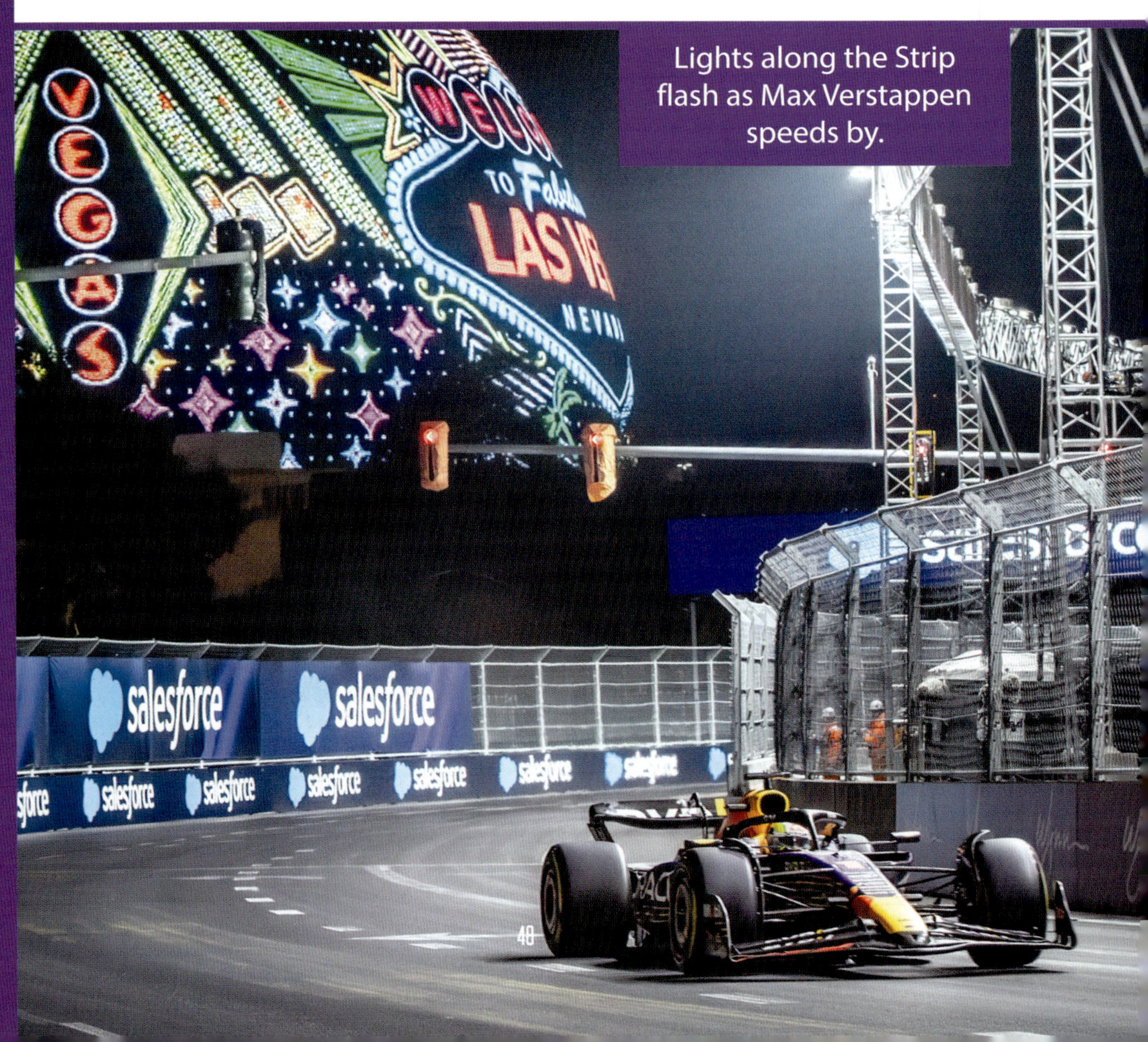

Lights along the Strip flash as Max Verstappen speeds by.

Drivers race along the streets of Las Vegas.

The official name for the raceway is the Las Vegas Strip Circuit. It opened for the first time in 2023. During race time, the curbs of the Strip are decorated with diamonds, clubs, spades, and hearts, representing a casino theme.

Before construction began on the Las Vegas Strip Circuit, more than 30 layout options were presented for the street track. Once a course was decided, the city of Las Vegas had to make some changes to its roads to make them safe for high-speed racing. New pavement was laid, street lights were added, and space was made for grandstands, garages, and pit areas.

After months of preparation, the first Las Vegas Grand Prix was held in November 2023. It saw a top racing speed of 227.4 miles per hour (366 kmh).

TRACK STATS

- **Year opened**: 2023
- **Length**: 3.6 miles (6 km)
- **Number of laps in the race**: 50
- **Number of turns**: 17

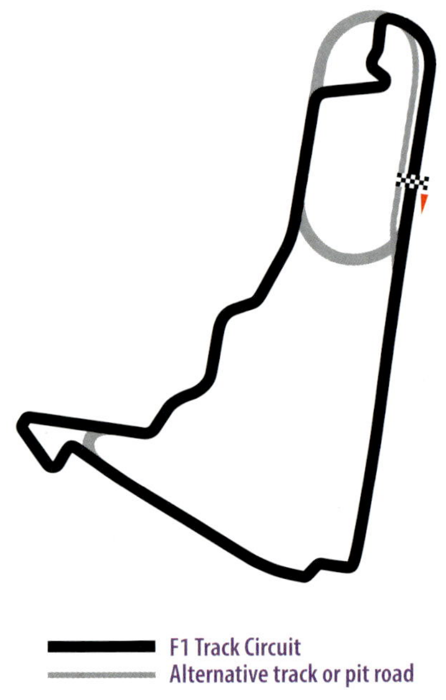

MEXICO CITY GRAND PRIX

The Mexico City Grand Prix is held at the Autódromo Hermanos Rodríguez circuit. It is known for its high-altitude location, 7,497 feet (2,285 m) above sea level. Being at a high elevation means the oxygen is thinner, which makes it harder to breathe. The higher altitude can also affect a car's performance, making races on this track extra-challenging.

Construction for this track began in 1959, and the raceway was completed at the end of that year. It held Mexico's first

Fans watch from the grandstands as George Russell races by.

Formula 1 Championship race in 1963. More than 50 years later, the track was updated with three new corners. Some sections were also rebuilt, but the overall shape of the track stayed the same. When the track reopened to host its first race after its renovation, about 240,000 spectators showed up to catch the excitement.

TRACK STATS

- **Year opened**: 1959
- **Length**: 2.7 miles (4 km)
- **Number of laps in the race**: 71
- **Number of turns**: 17

FUN FACT

The Mexico City Grand Prix is held in Mexico City, which sits in what was once Lake Texcoco. The lake was drained in order to build the city.

Lando Norris competes for McLaren at the Mexico City Grand Prix.

MIAMI GRAND PRIX

The Miami Grand Prix is a newer race in Formula 1. It was first held in 2022. The street circuit takes place at the Miami International Autodrome, located along the city's coastline.

It took several years for Formula 1 to get approval to build a racetrack in Miami. Multiple locations were proposed, but local residents did not want construction near their homes. Finally in 2021, it was agreed that the track would be built around the Hard Rock Stadium, which is the home of the Miami Dolphins football team.

TRACK STATS

- **Year opened**: 2022
- **Length**: 3.4 miles (5 km)
- **Number of laps in the race**: 57
- **Number of turns**: 19

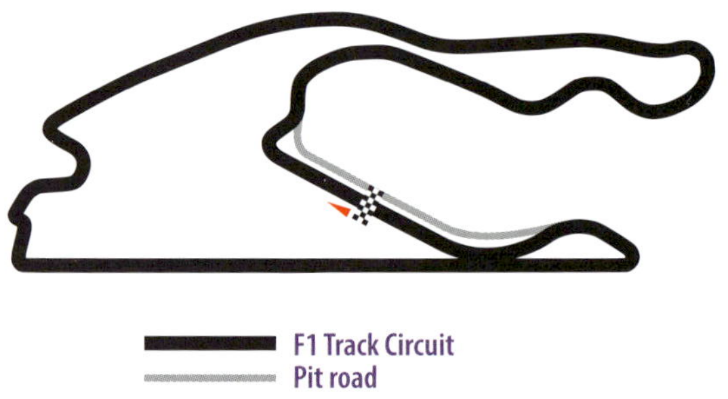

Max Verstappen competes for Red Bull Racing at the Miami Grand Prix.

Miami International Autodrome

FUN FACT

There is a mock marina in the middle of the track. The boats sit on top of the ground which is painted to look like water.

Construction on the Miami International Autodrome started in April 2021, and the entire complex was ready for the 2022 Formula 1 racing season. The track is a combination raceway. Part of it is permanent track and part is street circuit. Race cars can travel up to 199 miles per hour (320 kmh). The first Miami Grand Prix at the Autodrome in 2022 proved to be a success.

MONACO GRAND PRIX

The Monaco Grand Prix is a historic Formula 1 race. It takes place on the Circuit de Monaco, a track that opened in 1929 in the district of Monte Carlo. In 1950, the Circuit de Monaco became the second circuit to host Formula 1 races. At the time, Silverstone in the United Kingdom was the only other circuit to hold F1 races.

Unlike many other tracks that have changed over the years, the Circuit de Monaco has stayed almost the same. It has a narrow, winding layout that weaves through the streets of the city, which is located on the coast of the Mediterranean Sea.

FUN FACT

The Hairpin is the slowest corner in Formula 1 racing. Drivers have to go around 30 miles per hour (48 kmh) and steer carefully to avoid a crash.

The Hairpin

Preparations for the Monaco Grand Prix start about seven weeks before the main event. More than 20 miles (32 km) of barriers are built around the district, along with thousands of feet of fencing. Then grandstands for spectators are installed along the raceway.

The Monaco Grand Prix is just under 162 miles (261 km) long. Formula 1 requires races to be at least 190 miles (306 km) long, but an exception is made for the historic Monaco Grand Prix. The race is also one of only three circuits in F1 history that has a tunnel. Tunnels can be challenging for drivers. The change of light can make it hard to see. Tunnels can also affect the aerodynamics of a car.

Charles Leclerc races along the streets of Monaco.

TRACK STATS

- **Year opened**: 1929
- **Length**: 2.1 miles (3 km)
- **Number of laps in the race**: 78
- **Number of turns**: 19

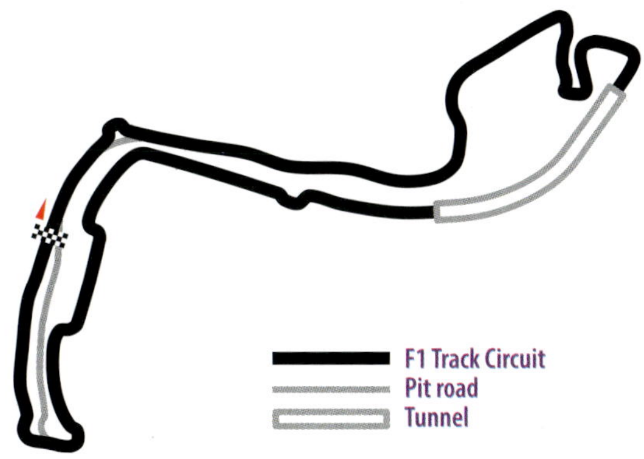

QATAR GRAND PRIX

The Qatar Grand Prix was first held in 2021. It takes place at the Lusail International Circuit in the Middle Eastern country of Qatar. The circuit was built in little more than one year with a crew of more than 1,000 people. It started out hosting motorcycle races when it first opened in 2004. By 2006, it hosted its first car race, a series that was known as the GP Masters.

The Qatar Grand Prix is one of the few Formula 1 races to be held

FUN FACT

The artificial grass surrounding the Lusail International Circuit helps prevent desert sands from blowing onto the track.

The Lusail International Circuit is known for night races.

In 2023, six F1 races were held at night in Qatar, Singapore, Bahrain, Saudi Arabia, Abu Dhabi, and Las Vegas.

at night. When lights were installed at the Lusail International Circuit in 2008 for nighttime events, the track was the largest lit event venue in the world with 3,600 bulbs shining over the venue. That record was later taken by the Yas Marina Circuit in Abu Dhabi.

TRACK STATS

- **Year opened**: 2004
- **Length**: 3.4 miles (5 km)
- **Number of laps in the race**: 57
- **Number of turns**: 16

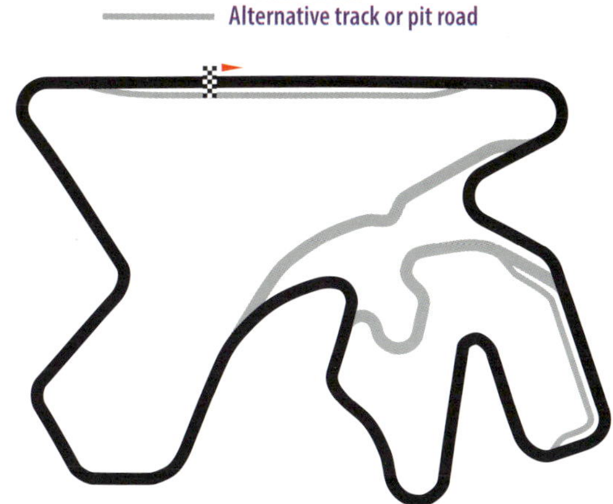

SÃO PAULO GRAND PRIX

The São Paulo Grand Prix takes place at Interlagos Circuit in São Paulo, Brazil. The track is more than 80 years old. Before the Interlagos Circuit was built, car races in São Paulo took place on the streets. This proved to be dangerous. Plans were made to build a permanent racetrack, and construction began in 1938. By November 1939, the track was ready, but it was very simple. At the time of its opening, there wasn't enough money to put in grandstands. They were built a few years later. Despite the lack of seats, about 15,000 people showed up to watch the first race called the Grand Prix of the City of São Paulo.

FUN FACT

Most Formula 1 races run clockwise, but the grand prix races of Azerbaijan, Singapore, United States (Austin), Abu Dhabi, and São Paulo run counter-clockwise.

Valtteri Bottas competes for Alfa Romeo Racing at the São Paulo Grand Prix.

Interlagos Circuit

The Interlagos Circuit is in an area with unpredictable weather. It rains a lot during races, which can be dangerous for drivers. In 1967, the track was closed to major renovations to meet new safety standards. By 1970, it was reopened, and three years later, São Paulo hosted its first Formula 1 race. It has hosted the Grand Prix in Brazil every year since then.

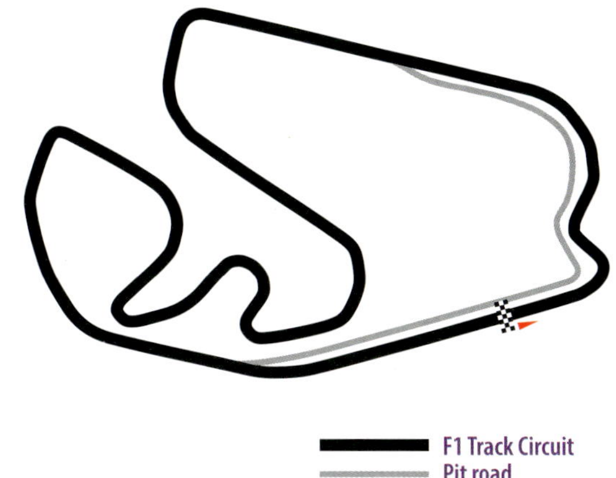

TRACK STATS

- **Year opened**: 1940
- **Length**: 2.7 miles (4 km)
- **Number of laps in the race**: 71
- **Number of turns**: 15

SAUDI ARABIA GRAND PRIX

The Jeddah Corniche Circuit is home to the Saudi Arabia Grand Prix. The circuit is located in Jeddah, a popular tourist area in Saudi Arabia. Building of the track started in 2021 and was finished in less than a year. The street circuit runs along the Red Sea and loops around a blue lagoon. It is the longest street circuit and the second-longest overall track in Formula 1 racing.

FUN FACT

Lewis Hamilton was the winner of the first Saudi Arabia Grand Prix held in 2021.

Lewis Hamilton races on the Jeddah Corniche Circuit.

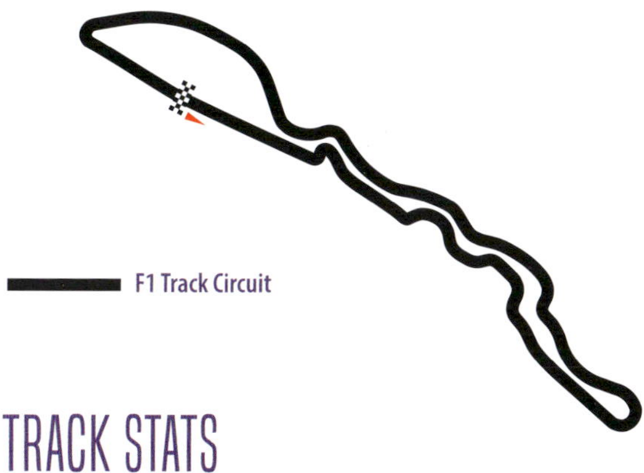

The Jeddah Corniche Circuit track has a unique shape. It is long and narrow, which can be a challenge for drivers, especially on the tight turns at the ends. But the track's shape also makes it fast. The track is the fastest street circuit in Formula 1 racing. Cars can hit 200 miles (322 km) per hour.

TRACK STATS

- **Year opened**: 2021
- **Length**: 3.8 miles (6 km)
- **Number of laps in the race**: 50
- **Number of turns**: 27

The Saudi Arabia Grand Prix is held at night to avoid the hot daytime temperatures in Jeddah, which can be 95 degrees Fahrenheit (35 degrees Celsius) or higher.

One of the most spectacular events at the Saudi Arabia Grand Prix is the fireworks display over the water after the race.

SINGAPORE GRAND PRIX

The Singapore Grand Prix was the first Formula 1 race to be held at night. The race takes place on the streets of Singapore. Singapore is both a city and a country, made up of one main island and 62 smaller islets.

The course is officially called the Marina Bay Street Circuit. Before race time, the circuit lights up against the city skyline, which is packed with skyscrapers that sit along a large bay.

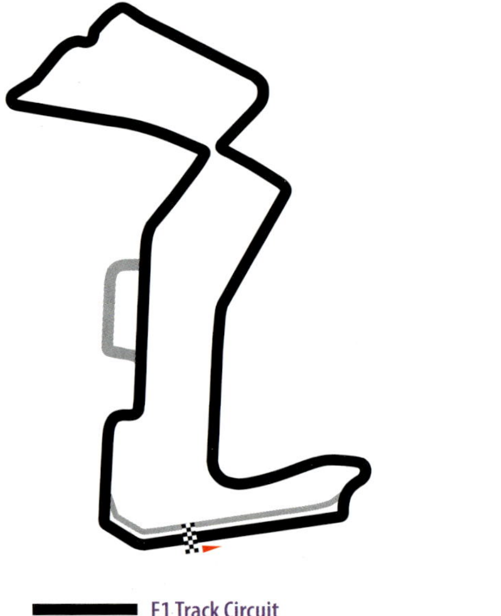

F1 Track Circuit
Alternative track, service road, or pit road

TRACK STATS

- **Year opened**: 2008
- **Length**: 3.1 miles (5 km)
- **Number of laps in the race**: 61
- **Number of turns**: 19

Ferrari takes the lead during a Singapore Grand Prix.

The Marina Bay Street Circuit runs near the Singapore Flyer, one of the largest observation wheels in the world.

Since this track is in the middle of a densely populated city, it takes five months to set up for the event. Fencing and trusses are built, light projectors are brought in, and barriers are placed along the route. To keep the Marina Bay Street Circuit lit up for the race, 1,600 lights are used. The lights are custom-made and are four times brighter than lights at regular sports stadiums. When the race is over, it takes about two months to remove the extra infrastructure from around the city.

The street track itself winds under one bridge and over another, passes Singapore's city hall, and at one point goes under the grandstands. Since Singapore is a very hot and humid country, the pit crews for the F1 cars have to keep an eye on moisture buildup and temperature of each car.

FUN FACT

Due to the heat and humidity along with the course's bumpy surface and 19 turns, the Singapore Grand Prix is considered one of the more challenging races in Formula 1.

SPANISH GRAND PRIX

The Circuit de Barcelona-Catalunya began hosting the Spanish Grand Prix in 1991, the same year it was built. The raceway is made up of fast and slow corners and several elevation changes.

While this track was under construction, the City of Barcelona was also preparing to host the 1992 Summer Olympics. During those Olympic Games, the Circuit de Barcelona-Catalunya was used as a start and finishing point for Olympic cyclists.

FUN FACT

The Circuit de Barcelona-Catalunya is configured so that a tight turn corner can be added to make it more challenging.

Charles Leclerc, competing for Ferrari, takes the lead.

Cars begin racing at the start of the Spanish Grand Prix.

Today, the Circuit is often used for car testing and driver practice during Formula 1's offseason in the winter. Barcelona usually has pleasant weather during this time of year. This makes it an ideal location for drivers and teams to prepare for the Formula 1 season ahead. As a result, many drivers are familiar with the track at the Circuit de Barcelona-Catalunya.

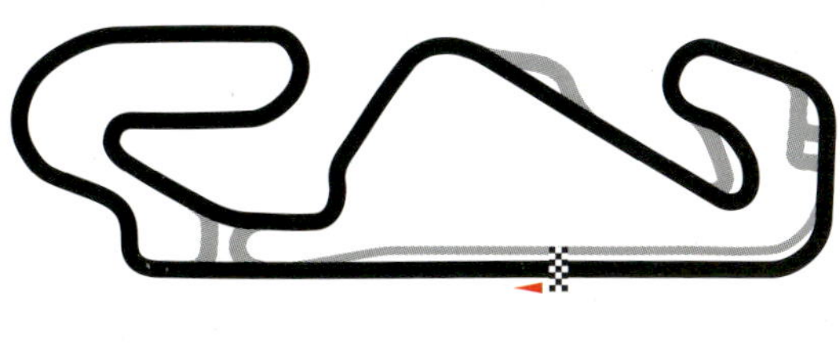

F1 Track Circuit
Alternative track, service road, or pit road

TRACK STATS

- **Year opened**: 1991
- **Length**: 2.9 miles (5 km)
- **Number of laps in the race**: 66
- **Number of turns**: 16

UNITED STATES GRAND PRIX

The United States Grand Prix is held at the Circuit of the Americas in Austin, Texas. The first United States Grand Prix was held in 1908 on regular streets in Georgia. The first time it was held on a track was in 1958 at the Riverside International Raceway. The Circuit of the Americas is the 10th location for the race. NASCAR races are held here too.

The Circuit of the Americas, also known as

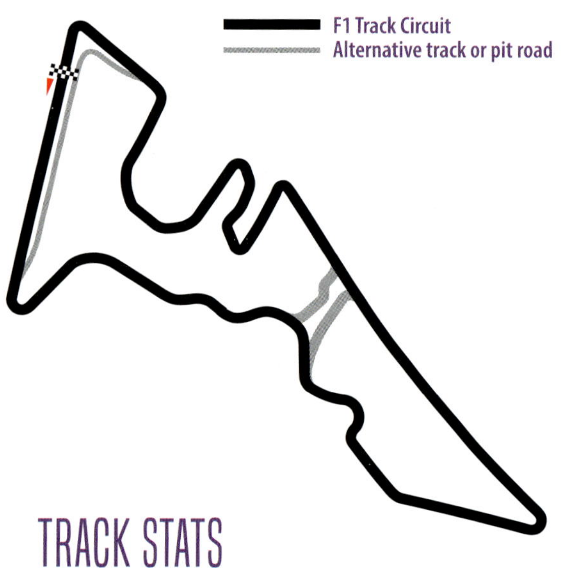

TRACK STATS

- **Year opened**: 2012
- **Length**: 3.4 miles (5 km)
- **Number of laps in the race**: 56
- **Number of turns**: 20

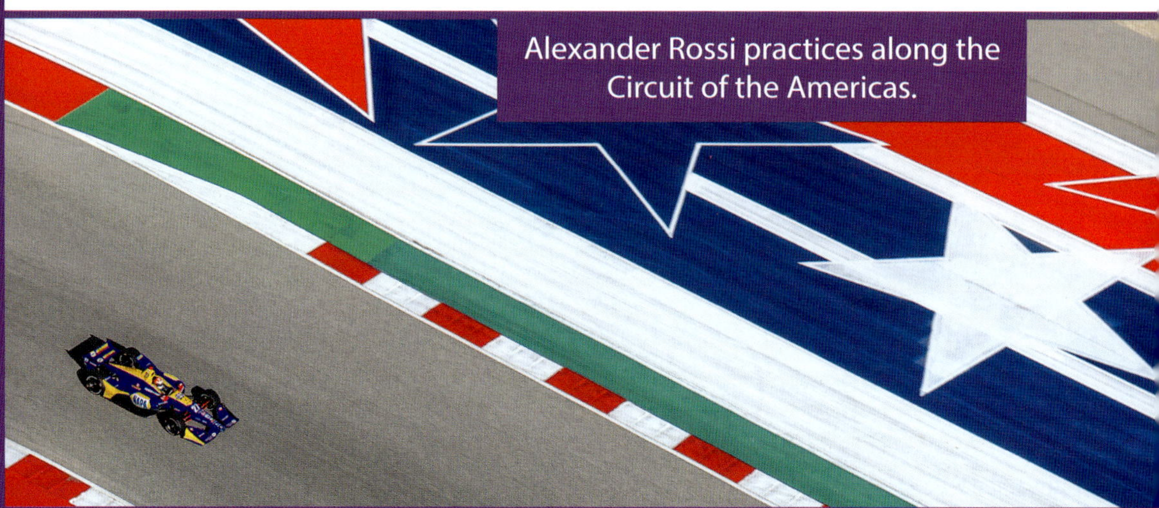

Alexander Rossi practices along the Circuit of the Americas.

COTA, has numerous curves and two sharp turns. Its designers were inspired by other tracks around the world, such as Silverstone in England. Like the Interlagos Circuit in São Paulo, the Circuit of the Americas also runs counterclockwise.

Construction took longer than was expected, but the track was completed just in time for the 2012 Formula 1 season. It was officially completed on September 21, 2012, and the track opened on October 21, 2012. Legendary Driver Mario Andretti drove a ceremonial first lap on opening day.

The circuit is built on soil that has a lot of clay in it. As the track has settled over time, it has shifted. This has caused the track to become bumpy, which can be dangerous for drivers. The track has had to be resurfaced and repaired several times.

Cars begin racing at the United States Grand Prix.

FUN FACT

Though the Circuit of the Americas also holds races for other motor series, it was specially built to accommodate Formula 1 racing. It's the first raceway in the United States to do so.

FORMULA 2

Formula 2, or F2, is the second-highest tier of Formula 1 racing. It is an important stepping stone for young drivers on a path to reaching Formula 1. F2 began as a way to offer less experienced drivers the chance to race on international circuits and compete in similar cars as Formula 1 drivers. Formula 2 has become a training ground for potential Formula 1 drivers.

FUN FACT

The first organized Formula 2 race took place in 1948 at the Monza Circuit in Italy.

The race as it is organized today has been running since 2017. Formula 2 typically has about 10 teams, and,

Theo Pourchaire *(5)* of ART Racing and Oliver Bearman *(8)* of Prema Racing lead the field in a F2 race.

F2 drivers race in Monza, Italy.

like Formula 1, each team has two drivers. The teams are often supported by Formula 1 teams.

There are usually 28 races in a Formula 2 season. The races happen over 12 weekends throughout the year and follow the same calendar as the F1 races. There are two F2 races that happen early in the day, preceding the main event of the F1 race.

FORMULA 1: F.Y.I.

The cars used in Formula 2 are not as powerful as the Formula 1 cars. The top speed for an F2 car is under 200 miles per hour (322 kmh). Formula 1 cars can go more than 230 miles per hour (370 kmh).

FORMULA 3

Formula 3 is the third tier of Formula racing, coming under Formula 2 and Formula 1 on the motorsport ladder. Like F2, it is a stepping stone for young and up-and-coming drivers where they can hone their skills and prepare for higher tiers of car racing. The F3 racing series started in 2019.

Like F2, F3 races happen during Formula 1 race weekends, but F3 races begin on Friday and continue on Saturday and Sunday.

Formula 3 cars are the slowest in the Formula series. They go up to 168 miles per hour (270 kmh). There are 10 teams in Formula 3, and each team has three drivers. This is different from F1 and F2 teams, which only have two drivers per team.

FUN FACT

With three drivers per team, there are 30 cars on the track at the same time during Formula 3 races. This makes for extra-close racing among drivers.

Christian Mansell (24) competes in an F3 race in Monza, Italy.

ALFA ROMEO 158

The Italian-made Alfa Romeo 158 was first introduced to racing in 1938. It made its Formula 1 debut in 1947. The Alfa Romeo 158, also known as the Alfetta, won 47 of 55 Grand Prix events during its Formula 1 competition years. It still holds the record for one of the most winning Formula 1 cars ever.

The "158" in the car's name comes from the fact that it had a 1.5-liter engine with eight cylinders. This is known today as a V8 engine. The look of this car has been described as a torpedo for its long, rounded shape. On the inside, the car's seat was meant to resemble a comfortable armchair, and the steering wheel was made of wood.

FUN FACT

Alfetta means "little alfa" in Italian—a perfect name for the pint-sized Alfa Romeo 158.

FERRARI 312B2

In 1971, the Ferrari 312B2 became the first F1 car to use racing slicks—race car tires that are completely smooth. Smooth tires had already been used in drag racing, but never in F1. The smooth surface of these tires allows race cars to have better grip, or traction, on the ground when the track is dry. The nose of the Ferrari 312B2 was also square-shaped, a new look for cars at the time. The car made its debut at the Monaco Grand Prix and won four races in its first season. It was driven by legendary Mario Andretti and two other F1 drivers.

There were only four of these Ferraris built in the 1970s and a total of five drivers that raced the car. The Ferrari 312B2 won its last Grand Prix in South Africa in 1973. It was soon retired in favor of newer models.

LOTUS 25

The Lotus 25 car was built for the 1963 Formula 1 racing season. It was the first F1 car to have a monocoque chassis, which is a type of construction method where the outer part of a vehicle, the frame, is a single piece and carries the structure of the car. *Monocoque* means "single shell." This new design made the Lotus 25 stronger and lighter than any other F1 car at the time. It also had better fuel economy and was lower and narrower than other cars on the track.

All of these features gave the car an advantage in competition—being light, narrow, and more fuel-efficient allowed the car to move fast. F1 driver Jim Clark won 14 World Champion Grand Prix races in the Lotus 25.

FUN FACT

The idea for the monocoque chassis structure of Lotus 25 was first drawn on a napkin by Colin Chapman, a legendary car engineer and the owner of Lotus Cars.

LOTUS 72

The Lotus 72 won 20 Grand Prix victories during its time on the racetracks. It was one of the fastest and the lightest F1 cars ever made. The car made its Formula 1 debut in 1970 at the Spanish Grand Prix. It had a unique look for the time, with a very sleek front-end design. It was also the first F1 car to have side-mounted radiators instead of nose-mounted radiators. The radiators are responsible for moving heat from the coolant liquid so the coolant can do its job—cool the car. The Lotus 72 was used in F1 racing from 1970 to 1975.

MERCEDES-BENZ F1 W05 HYBRID

In 2014, hybrids—cars that run on both fuel and electricity—were allowed to compete in Formula 1 for the first time, but they had to meet strict FIA requirements. Only three carmakers were able to meet the requirements in time to build cars for the 2014 season: Mercedes, Ferrari, and Renault. The Mercedes F1 W05 Hybrid was driven by legendary driver Lewis Hamilton in its debut season. Hamilton had a successful year driving the car, winning four Grand Prix races.

The use of hybrid engines showed that the F1 organization was forward-thinking when it came not only to new technologies, but also to sustainability. The engine/battery combination is called

FORMULA 1: F.Y.I.

Hybrid F1 cars generate electricity through an Energy Recovery System (ERS). Energy generated by the use of the brakes and exhaust system is converted by the ERS into electricity. The electricity is used to power the electric motor or it is stored in a battery for use later.

a power unit in Formula 1. Though hybrids are not as loud as traditional cars, they are powerful, generating more power than their fuel-only counterparts.

MERCEDES-BENZ W 196

The Mercedes-Benz W 196 made its Formula 1 debut in 1954. Its top speed was 190 miles per hour (306 kmh). At the time, this car used the most advanced technology in racing. It had a light frame, specialty breaks, and a streamlined body to help with aerodynamics.

At the 1954 race in Remis, France, there were two Mercedes-Benz W 196 cars competing. The drivers of those cars, Juan Manuel Fangio and Stirling Moss, won first and second place. Fangio ended the season as the 1954 F1 World Champion.

The Mercedes-Benz W 196 only raced for two years before it was retired. During the 1954 and 1955 seasons, the car won 9 of the 12 races it competed in.

RENAULT RS01

The Renault RS01 was the first Formula 1 car to be powered by a turbocharged engine. Today, turbocharged engines are common in many types of cars, but before the 1970s, they did not exist. A turbocharger helps the car's main engine generate more power and have better driving performance. BMW, Honda, and Porche soon followed the Renault RS01 with turbocharged engines of their own.

FUN FACT

The Renault RS01 appears in the *Formula 1 Championship Edition* video game.

The Renault RS01 made its Formula 1 debut at the 1977 British Grand Prix. Only four cars were built, and they won a total of 20 Grand Prix races. At first, however, people were surprised by its bright yellow color and the whistling sound it made when in motion. Due to its whistling, the car was nicknamed "the teapot." The car also had some performance problems such as an engine that would overheat. The problems were fixed over time, but the cars were retired after the 1979 season.

TYRRELL 019

When the Tyrrell 019 made its debut on the Formula 1 track in 1990, it had a significant new feature: an elevated nose cone. The elevated nose cone soon became the inspiration for better aerodynamic race car design among other F1 cars.

The designers of this car realized that the lower nose cone affected the airflow around the Tyrrell 018 race car. They decided to raise the nose as a way to allow more and faster airflow underneath the car. The faster movement of air meant there was less pressure on the car, which allowed it to move faster. Though the Tyrrell 019 introduced this major advancement in race car design, it did not perform very well on the track. It was replaced by the Tyrrell 020 after just one season.

TYRRELL P34

The Tyrrell P34 was truly a unique race car for one major reason: it had six wheels. Four small wheels were placed on the front sides and two large wheels in the back. It was the first of its kind. The out-of-the-box design was kept top secret until the car debuted at the 1976 Spanish Grand Prix. Not even the drivers knew about the Tyrrell P34's extra tires.

Another unique feature of this car was its portholes found on either side of the steering wheel. The windows were much like the small round windows found on a boat. Due to the design of this car, drivers were not able to see their front tires. The portholes were created to make those tires visible. The Tyrrell P34 had some success early on, but in 1983, the FIA decided to ban cars with more than four wheels.

2022 FORMULA 1 CARS

In 2022, all Formula cars were required to have a new feature: over-wheel winglets. These winglets go over the front tires and wheel covers. In the past, air from a car's tires would be "thrown" to an oncoming car. This would lessen that car's aerodynamics. With the winglets, air is directed over the tires and is streamlined along the sides of the car. This prevents the air from impeding other cars' aerodynamics.

The wheel covers, also known as hubcaps for regular street cars, rotate with each wheel. A hole on each cover releases hot air generated by the brakes. Like the winglets, this helps regulate where the air will flow, allowing for better car performance. The overall goal of both new additions was to allow cars to follow more closely behind each other without airflow getting in the way of any car's performance.

ALFA ROMEO C43

Alfa Romeo was established in 1910 and has been making race cars ever since. It competed in European racing competitions in the 1920s and 1930s. By the late 1940s, Alfa Romeo dominated European Grand Prix racing.

The 2023 Alfa Romeo C43 was unveiled with an all-new look. Previous Alfa Romeos were mostly white, but the 2023 model is all red and black. The black on the car is not paint, though. It's carbon fiber, which is used to make parts of the car. Keeping sections of the car unpainted helps reduce the weight of the vehicle.

ALPHATAURI AT03

AlphaTauri AT03 is a Formula 1 car designed and constructed by team Scuderia AlphaTauri. The 2023 model of this car features several advancements, many of which involve aerodynamics.

Safety features were also modified for the AlphaTauri AT03. The car has a longer nose to better protect the driver in case of a front impact. In addition, the chassis of the car was built to absorb more energy all-around, which better protects the driver and the fuel cell.

The 2023 AlphaTauri AT03 runs on a more sustainable "E10" fuel, 10 percent of which is made from renewable sources.

ALPINE A522

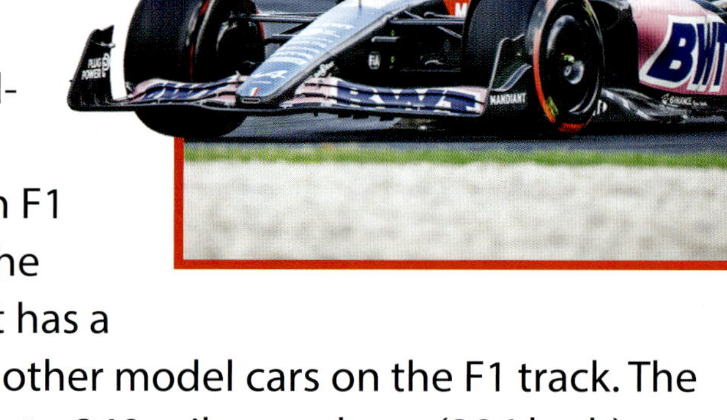

The Alpine A522 stands out with its bold pink-and-blue body. Designed and constructed by the French F1 team, Alpine, it is one of the fastest cars on the track. It has a higher nose compared to other model cars on the F1 track. The car can reach speeds of up to 240 miles per hour (386 kmh).

ASTON MARTIN AMR23

The Aston Martin AMR23 is built with a Mercedes engine. It has deep sidepods, areas on each side of the car that help regulate airflow around the back wheels, helping reduce drag so the car moves at top speed. The Aston Martin also has a flatter and wider nose than previous models. The shoulder right behind the driver's head was raised to make room for the Mercedes engine.

FERRARI SF-23

The 2022 F1 Ferrari SF-23 has improved aerodynamics, a more efficient power unit, and a new suspension. The shape of the front wing and nose were also updated on the 2022 model.

HAAS VF-23

The Haas VF-23 Formula 1 car features a wider engine cover and cockpit. Deeper sidepods on either side of the car allow for better aerodynamics and more efficient cooling of the car.

MCLAREN MCL60

The McLaren MCL60 was built with a tighter sidepod that takes up less space to make room for inlet tunnels that run underneath each side of the car. These tunnels allow air to flow smoothly. This model also has an expanded floor placement, which helps enhance downforce, increasing grip for the tires and allowing the car to go faster.

MERCEDES W14

When designing the Mercedes W14, the design team aimed to improve the car's aerodynamics. It also wanted to make the car more balanced while traveling at high speeds. As a result, the car's weight was reduced to make it as light as possible. A lighter chassis was used, and adjustments were made to the cooling system to make it more effective and efficient.

WILLIAMS FW45

Many of the upgrades made to the Williams FW45 happened to the car's floor, which was adjusted on the chassis to help better align the car as it's moving. In addition, new winglets direct the flow of air coming off the front of the car to the top of the body. From there, the air flows through the sidepods, which then funnel the air to the back corners and out of the car.

RED BULL RB19

The Red Bull RB19 is considered one of the most dominant cars in the history of Formula 1, winning 21 of the 22 races in the 2023 season. Part of the reason for its success might be that the RB19 is 44 pounds (20 kg) lighter than the previous model. Weight was reduced in as many parts of the car as possible.

Aerodynamics were closely looked at in the RB19's design. The car's deep sidepods increase the amount of air flowing down the sides of the car. In addition, the floor sits low on the RB19 and runs close to the track, which creates a large amount of downforce. This further enhances aerodynamics, handling, and speed.

Chief technical officer Adrian Newey is credited with designing this car's aerodynamics. Newey won the 2024 World Car Person of the Year for his design of the RB19.

FORMULA 2 AND FORMULA 3 CARS

All Formula 2 and Formula 3 cars are made by Italian race car manufacturer Dallara. The company also makes cars for the Indy500 and for the North American racing series known as INDYCAR.

The latest version of the Formula 2 car has improvements to the front wing and rear wings, mainly making them larger. The new design also allows for better airflow, particularly when the car is driving near other cars on the track.

Dallara's F2 cars are more powerful than Formula 3 cars but less powerful than F1 cars. Formula 2 cars have 620 horsepower V6 engines. Formula 3 cars also have V6 engines, but they are less powerful at 380 horsepower. F1 cars that have the most powerful engines with a little more than 1,000 horsepower.

Formula 2 car

Formula 3 car

Dallara's Formula 3 cars are known for being light and easy to maneuver. This, combined with the fact that their engines have a bit less power than the F2 models, makes the Dallara Formula 3 car perfect for up-and-coming drivers in motorsports.

All Formula 3 cars are alike, including their engines, which must be built the same. They are often sealed by race organizers so no team can tune their engine afterward. Since 2016, Mecachrome has been the supplier of all F3 engines.

FUN FACT

Formula 3 cars look similar to Formula 2 vehicles. The only real visual difference between the cars is the shape of the nose. The F2 cars have wider noses.

F1 STAR DRIVERS

MARIO ANDRETTI

There are few race car drivers that are as accomplished or as legendary as Mario Andretti. He was born in Italy in 1940, during World War II. During the war, Andretti and his family had to leave their home because it was no longer safe. They spent seven years in a camp for displaced persons. After the war ended in 1945, they left the camp and moved to a new home in Lucca, Italy.

It was in Lucca that Andretti discovered racing for the first time. In 1954, he went to the Italian Grand Prix. There, he saw numerous

FUN FACT

Mario Andretti is the only driver to win an Indianapolis 500, the Daytona 500, and the Formula 1 World Championship.

Andretti competes at the Dutch Grand Prix.

Formula 1 cars speeding around the track driven by some of F1's early drivers, including Juan Manuel Fangio and Alberto Ascari.

In 1955, Andretti's family moved to the United States. By age 18, he had gotten involved in motorsports. Andretti and his twin brother, Aldo, fixed up a Hudson Hornet and shared the car when racing at local tracks. In 1959, Aldo was in an accident and decided to stop racing, but Mario continued to build his racing career.

Andretti races in a Lotus-Ford.

DRIVER STATS

- **Country**: United States
- **Years Raced in Formula 1**: 1968 to 1982
- **World Championship Wins**: 1978
- **Number of Formula 1 Wins**: 12

Andretti competed in stock car and open-wheel racing. He won the Indianapolis 500 race numerous times. He also raced for the United States Auto Club and NASCAR, where he won the Daytona 500. Andretti made his Formula 1 debut in 1968. He drove for Formula 1 over the next eight years but only part-time. Finally in 1976, Andretti decided to sign on as a full-time driver. That year, he won the Japanese Grand Prix. Just two years later, he became a Formula 1 World Champion. From there, Andretti had a successful Formula 1 career and drove for the organization until 1982.

ALBERTO ASCARI

One of Formula 1's earliest drivers, Italian Alberto Ascari started racing motorcycles at age 19. He also ran his family's car garage business. When World War II started, the garage had to start servicing military vehicles. It was during the war that Ascari met another race car driver: Luigi Villoresi. By then, Ascari was married and had a family. He was not planning to go back to racing, but Villoresi convinced him to give it another try.

Ascari and Villoresi joined the Ferrari team, owned by family friend Enzo Ferrari. Soon after his return to racing, Ascari became the first Formula 1

DRIVER STATS

- **Country**: Italy
- **Years Raced in Formula 1**: 1950 to 1955
- **World Championship Wins**: 1952, 1953
- **Number of Formula 1 Wins**: 13

Ascari wins the British Grand Prix.

driver to win two championships in a row.

In 1955, Ascari lost control of his race car at the Monaco Grand Prix. He swerved into the Mediterranean Sea. He managed to escape his sinking car, surviving the accident. Just days later, Ascari attended a practice session to watch other drivers. While there, he decided to take a test drive himself, but on the third lap, he swerved and crashed his car. Ascari did not survive the accident. He was honored in his home country of Italy, and his racing legacy lives on.

FUN FACT

Alberto Ascari is the only Italian driver who has won two Formula 1 Championships. He drove a Ferrari in both of them.

Ascari races a Ferrari at the Silverstone Circuit.

FERNANDO ALONSO

Alonso celebrates his second place finish at the Canadian Grand Prix.

When Fernando Alonso won his first Formula 1 World Championship in 2005 at the age of 24, he was the youngest driver to do so. His passion for racing began with his father, Luis, who loved go-kart racing. Luis built Alonso a miniature Formula 1 car when he was three years old, and he has continued driving ever since. As Alonso got older and gained more experience, his father became his mechanic.

In 2002, at age 21, Alonso became a test driver for Formula 1, which gave him invaluable experience. The following year, he became the youngest Grand Prix winner ever at just 22 years old. Three years later, he won his first Formula 1 World Championship and did it again in 2006. Alonso has had an extensive racing career, and he continues to drive for Formula 1's Aston Martin team.

DRIVER STATS

- **Country**: Spain
- **Years Raced in Formula 1**: 2001 to present
- **World Championship Wins**: 2005, 2006
- **Number of Formula 1 Wins**: 32 (as of 2023)

JENSON BUTTON

British-born Jenson Button began racing go-karts at age eight. By age 11, Button was competing in a junior racing category known as the British Cadet.

After years of a successful go-karting career, Button received the opportunity to test drive a Formula 1 car. It was really a test to see if he could fill another driver's vacancy. Button's test drive was a success, and at 20 years old, he became a Formula 1 driver. During the 2009 season, Button won six races and the World Championship. He drove in F1 for 17 seasons, retiring at 36 years old in 2017.

FORMULA 1: F.Y.I.

Many professional race car drivers have a background in go-karting, a sport that kids can start at a young age. The skills learned while maneuvering a go-kart are the basic skills needed to drive a race car.

DRIVER STATS

- **Country**: United Kingdom
- **Years Raced in Formula 1**: 2000 to 2017
- **World Championship Wins**: 2009
- **Number of Formula 1 Wins**: 15

Button waves to fans before a race.

JACK BRABHAM

Jack Brabham grew up near Sydney, Australia, in the 1920s and 1930s. His father was a grocer, selling fruits and vegetables at the neighborhood store. Brabham did not show much interest in selling groceries, but he loved the delivery vehicles. He was eager to drive them himself and started doing so before he was even old enough to have a driver's license. At 15, Brabham decided to work in an automobile garage and later became an engineer.

It wasn't until Brabham was married with three kids that he started racing. He was introduced to racing by a friend. He proved

DRIVER STATS

- **Country**: Australia
- **Years Raced in Formula 1**: 1955 to 1970
- **World Championship Wins**: 1959, 1960, 1966
- **Number of Formula 1 Wins**: 14

Brabham has been featured on a postage stamp.

to have a lot of natural talent for the sport. In 1958, Brabham made his Formula 1 debut. Just one year later, he won the World Championship. Brabham repeated the victory the following year, then again in 1966 at 40 years old.

Brabham drove his last race at the South African Grand Prix at age 44. His three sons followed in his footsteps, also becoming race car drivers.

FUN FACT

In 1979, Brabham was honored with the title "Sir Jack Brabham" by the British monarchy in recognition for his contribution to motorsports.

Brabham's race car

Clark celebrates a win.

JIM CLARK

Motorsports were not something that Jim Clark was used to seeing in his Scottish hometown of Berwickshire, an area near the border with England. Clark grew up surrounded by sheep! But books and magazines brought the thrill of race cars to life. Clark would take his family's car for a spin in the field near his house in secret. Soon, he was allowed to drive tractors on the family farm. Around age 17, Clark got his first car, a Sunbeam Talbot. He started participating in local car competitions and was soon winning races.

DRIVER STATS

- **Country**: United Kingdom
- **Years Raced in Formula 1**: 1960 to 1968
- **World Championship Wins**: 1963, 1965
- **Number of Formula 1 Wins**: 25

At age 22, Clark's racing skills caught the eye of Formula 1 Lotus car owner Colin Chapman. Chapman invited Clark to race one of his cars in a Formula junior league. Clark raced well and was quickly put on Team Lotus to race in Formula 1. By 1963, Clark had won his first World Championship.

By 1968, Clark had won 25 Grand Prix races, breaking Juan Manuel Fangio's record. But the same year, he was in an accident at a race in Germany and did not survive. Clark is remembered as one of F1's best racers.

JUAN MANUEL FANGIO

Born on June 24, 1911, in Balcare, Argentina, Juan Manuel Fangio is considered one of the greatest race car drivers of all time. Fangio started his journey in racing as a mechanic. Learning the ins and outs of cars gave him an advantage when he started racing for Formula 1.

Fangio's career spanned seven Formula 1 seasons, during which he won the World Championship title a record five times. This record was held for 46 years. It was broken by Michael Schumacher in 2003 when he won his sixth F1 Championship.

DRIVER STATS

- **Country**: Argentina
- **Years Raced in Formula 1**: 1950 to 1951; 1953 to 1958
- **World Championship Wins**: 1951, 1954, 1955, 1956, 1957
- **Number of Formula 1 Wins**: 24

Fangio drives his Mercedes Silver Arrow.

GIUSEPPE "NINO" FARINA

Born on October 30, 1906, in Turin, Italy, Guiseppe "Nino" Farina grew up among cars. His family owned a body shop and a business that designed Italian sports cars. At age 16, he rode along with his uncle in a car race. Farina's passion for motorsports was ignited.

Farina often crashed in his early races, but his talent caught the eye of racing team owner Enzo Ferrari, who recruited him to drive for the Scuderia Ferrari Alfa Romeo team. In 1950, Farina won the first-ever Formula 1 World Championship.

Farina continued racing for five more years until his retirement. In 1966, he was killed in a car accident on his way to watch the French Grand Prix.

Farina waves to fans after winning the International Trophy Race.

DRIVER STATS

- **Country**: Italy
- **Years Raced in Formula 1**: 1950 to 1955
- **World Championship Wins**: 1950
- **Number of Formula 1 Wins**: 5

EMERSON FITTIPALDI

Brazilian racing legend Emerson Fittipaldi was born in São Paulo, Brazil, in 1946. He was named after American writer Ralph Waldo Emerson. Like his father, who was a motorsports journalist, Fittipaldi also became a motorsports fan and soon decided he wanted to race cars.

Fueled by their passion for racing, Fittipaldi and his brother built and raced go-karts. Fittipaldi was a natural racer. In 1969, he went to England, not speaking any English. Fittipaldi raced in Formula 3 and Formula 2 and made his Formula 1 debut in 1970. Just two years later in 1972, he was a World Champion. In 1974, he won the title for a second time. Later in his career, Fittipaldi became an IndyCar driver.

FUN FACT

Emerson Fittipaldi's grandson Enzo is also a car racer. He drives for the Formula 2 series.

DRIVER STATS

- **Country**: Brazil
- **Years Raced in Formula 1**: 1970 to 1980
- **World Championship Wins**: 1972, 1974
- **Number of Formula 1 Wins**: 14

MIKA HAKKINEN

Mika Hakkinen began go-karting at the age five near his home just outside of Helsinki, Finland. By the time Hakkinen was 18 years old, he was a go-karting champion.

FUN FACT

Mika Hakkinen was nicknamed "Flying Finn" for the way his race car launched off the ground.

Soon, Hakkinen was racing for Formula 3, followed by Formula 2. By 1993, he was racing in Formula 1. He started as a test driver for Team Lotus. His talent was clear, and the owner of Team McLaren recognized this quickly and signed Hakkinen on to the team. In 1995, an accident took Hakkinen off the track for a while. He had a long, difficult recovery but was able to make a comeback. By 1998, Hakkinen won his first World Championship and won a second the following year.

DRIVER STATS

- **Country**: Finland
- **Years Raced in Formula 1**: 1991 to 2001
- **World Championship Wins**: 1998, 1999
- **Number of Formula 1 Wins**: 20

Hakkinen at the Japanese Grand Prix

MIKE HAWTHORN

Mike Hawthorn was Great Britain's first World Champion race car driver. Racing was familiar to Hawthorn. His father owned a car garage where he prepared race cars and motorcycles for competitions. With encouragement from his father, Hawthorn began racing motorcycles and won his first race at age 18. Three years later, he switched to car racing.

By 1953, when Hawthorn was 26 years old, he became a new member of the Enzo Ferrari Formula 1 team. He only won one race his first year at the 1953 French Grand Prix. Hawthorn struggled to come out on top in the years that followed due to an accident that left him burned. He was also grieving his father's death. But Hawthorn persisted, and his hard work paid off. Five years later, in 1958, he won a World Championship.

DRIVER STATS

- **Country**: United Kingdom
- **Years Raced in Formula 1**: 1952 to 1958
- **World Championship Wins**: 1958
- **Number of Formula 1 Wins**: 3

Hawthorn drives a Ferrari at the British Grand Prix.

LEWIS HAMILTON

It takes a legendary race car driver to win seven World Championships, and that is exactly what Lewis Hamilton has done. Only one other Formula 1 driver, Michael Schumacher, has won as many championships.

Hamilton was born in England in 1985. When he was eight, he was given a used go-kart, and by age 10, he was a go-karting champion.

Hamilton stands at the podium after winning the Saudi Arabia Grand Prix.

At a go-karting awards ceremony, Hamilton saw the head of a Formula 1 team, Ron Dennis. Hamilton told Dennis he wanted to race for his F1 team one day. Dennis gave Hamilton his phone number and a note that read, "Call me in nine years."

DRIVER STATS

- **Country**: United Kingdom
- **Years Raced in Formula 1**: 2007 to present
- **World Championship Wins**: 2008, 2014, 2015, 2017, 2018, 2019, 2020
- **Number of Formula 1 Wins**: 103 (as of 2023)

But Hamilton did not have to wait nine years. Three years after winning his go-karting award, he received a call from Dennis. He offered to support Hamilton's racing career if he continued to do well in school. Hamilton did well in both. He won eight more go-karting championships and had other major racing wins. By 2007, Lewis Hamilton was racing for Formula 1. Just a year later, he won his first of seven World Championships.

FUN FACT

In 2023, Lewis Hamilton earned his 103rd career win in Formula 1. That was more wins than all other drivers in 2023 combined.

Hamilton racing for Mercedes

DAMON HILL

British driver Damon Hill grew up in London around race car drivers, which included his father, Graham Hill. Tragically, Graham Hill died in an airplane crash along with a few other members of his Formula 1 racing team. Damon was just 11 years old, but he knew he wanted to be a racer too. After college, Hill started racing for Formula 3 and eventually became a test driver for Formula 1 in 1991. A year later, he made his official Formula 1 debut.

After four years of racing, Hill won his first and only World Championship. Hill had victories on and off throughout his Formula career. He decided to make 1999 his final season. He left racing with a respectable 22 wins, 2 driving titles, and a World Championship.

Damon Hill with the Belgian Grand Prix trophy

FORMULA 1: F.Y.I.

After retiring from Formula 1, Hill pursued another passion: music. He even once played guitar with former Beatles band member George Harrison.

DRIVER STATS

- **Country**: United Kingdom
- **Years Raced in Formula 1**: 1992 to 1999
- **World Championship Wins**: 1996
- **Number of Formula 1 Wins**: 22

GRAHAM HILL

Before becoming a race car driver, Graham Hill played a number of other sports. He also played music and was a member of Great Britain's Royal Navy. When Hill was 24 years old, he drove a Formula 3 car for the first time. Five years later, in 1958, he was ready for Formula 1. By 1962, Hill won his first championship after winning the Grand Prix in Italy, South Africa, Germany, and the Netherlands.

As he continued with his career, Hill became comfortable with the media and spoke about F1 racing, which helped to promote the sport. After stepping away from Formula 1 for a time, Hill had success driving in the United States, where he won the Indianapolis 500 in 1966. But he decided to return to Formula racing and rejoined in 1967. Just a year later, Hill won his second F1 World Championship title.

DRIVER STATS

- **Country**: United Kingdom
- **Years Raced in Formula 1**: 1958 to 1975
- **World Championship Wins**: 1962, 1968
- **Number of Formula 1 Wins**: 14

Graham Hill drives his car in celebration after winning the Monaco Grand Prix.

PHIL HILL

Hill wins the Italian Grand Prix.

Phil Hill, who was unrelated to Graham and Damon Hill, was born in Miami, Florida, in 1927. He was the first American to become a Formula 1 World Champion. When he was 12 years old, his aunt gave him a Model T Ford. He would often take it apart and put it back together to learn how the car worked.

DRIVER STATS

- **Country**: United States
- **Years Raced in Formula 1**: 1958 to 1964; 1966
- **World Championship Wins**: 1961
- **Number of Formula 1 Wins**: 3

Hill went to college for two years, but he left to work in a mechanic shop in Los Angeles, California. In 1947, he got a small car that he fixed up and started racing. Later, he was able to buy a Ferrari and continued to develop his racing skills. By 1958, at the age of 31, Hill joined Formula 1's Ferrari racing team. He was added to the roster after the deaths of two other Ferrari drivers.

Three years after joining the Ferrari team, Hill won the 1961 Formula 1 Championship, but it was a difficult moment. During the race, another driver and 14 spectators were killed in an accident. Hill won the race by just one point.

DENNY HULME

When Denny Hulme was just six years old, he learned how to drive a truck by sitting on his father's lap while they drove around their family farm in New Zealand. By age 17, Hulme was a mechanic and a driver, moving cargo long distances. It was good training for his future as a racer, especially since he drove many of New Zealand's winding roads.

In 1959, Hulme and his dad bought a car that they fixed up for racing. Hulme soon moved to London to further his career, and in 1964, he joined Formula 1. He won a World Championship in 1967, but he was always uncomfortable with the fame and attention that came with winning. After witnessing a number of accidents after his win, Hulme decided to leave Formula 1, but he kept racing elsewhere for almost 20 years.

DRIVER STATS

- **Country**: New Zealand
- **Years Raced in Formula 1**: 1965 to 1974
- **World Championship Wins**: 1967
- **Number of Formula 1 Wins**: 8

JAMES HUNT

James Hunt saw his first race at England's Silverstone Circuit when he was 18 years old. That was when he decided he would become a race car driver, determined to win a World Championship.

Hunt bought an old car and took two years to prepare it for racing. He did not have much early success in racing, but by 1974, he was competing in Formula 1. The following year, he won the Dutch Grand Prix. In 1976, he was asked to fill Emerson Fittipaldi's seat, as he had recently left Team McLaren for another team. It was a lucky break, as Hunt won the World Championship that year.

Hunt at the International Trophy race

FUN FACT

In 2013, a movie called *Rush* came to the big screen. It was a story about the rivalry between Hunt and teammate Niki Lauda when they raced for Formula 1 in the 1970s.

DRIVER STATS

- **Country**: United Kingdom
- **Years Raced in Formula 1**: 1973 to 1979
- **World Championship Wins**: 1976
- **Number of Formula 1 Wins**: 10

ALAN JONES

A native of Melbourne, Australia, Alan Jones got his start in racing through go-karting and was a champion by age 15.

In 1970, at 24 years old, Jones moved to London to pursue his racing career in Europe, the center of Formula 1 racing. Five years later, he began racing in Formula 1 and was fifth overall in his first season. He drove for two teams, and in 1978, he joined Williams Racing. Two years later, Jones won Grand Prix races in Britain, Canada, France, Argentina, and the United States and became the 1980 World Champion.

Jones wins the British Grand Prix.

DRIVER STATS

- **Country:** Australia
- **Years Raced in Formula 1**: 1975 to 1981; 1983; 1985 to 1986
- **World Championship Wins**: 1980
- **Number of Formula 1 Wins**: 12

NIKI LAUDA

Though Niki Lauda came from a wealthy family, his father did not agree with his choice to be a driver and refused to help him financially. Lauda did not give up. He borrowed money and enrolled in racing school. In 1968, he started racing for Formula 3 and made his way to Formula 2 by 1972. Lauda was 23 years old. Two years later, he started driving for Formula 1. Lauda won his first World Championship in 1975, just one year after joining F1. Two more World Championships followed, in 1977 and 1984.

DRIVER STATS

- **Country**: Austria
- **Years Raced in Formula 1**: 1971 to 1979; 1982 to 1985
- **World Championship Wins**: 1975, 1977, 1984
- **Number of Formula 1 Wins**: 25

FUN FACT

In 1976, Niki Lauda was in an accident that caused major burns to his face. That did not stop him from continuing to race. He won two of his three World Championships after his accident.

Lauda at the Belgian Grand Prix

NIGEL MANSELL

When Nigel Mansell was seven years old, he saw a Grand Prix race for the first time. He loved watching the race and wanted to do the same thing. He was soon competing in go-kart races. His path to Formula 1 racing came after earning a degree in aerospace engineering.

Mansell first drove for Formula Ford, an entry level racing league. In 1977, he won the Formula Ford Championship, even though he had a broken neck. A few days earlier, Mansell was in an accident while doing a test drive. Doctors told him he could never race again, but he didn't listen. Mansell sneaked out of the hospital and continued racing anyway.

Mansell joined Formula 1 in 1980. He had on and off success until 1992, when he won the World Championship. His last year of Formula 1 racing was 1995.

Mansell celebrates winning the Drivers' Championship.

DRIVER STATS

- **Country**: United Kingdom
- **Years Raced in Formula 1**: 1980 to 1992; 1994 to 1995
- **World Championship Wins**: 1992
- **Number of Formula 1 Wins**: 31

NELSON PIQUET

Growing up, Nelson Piquet's parents wanted him to pursue the sport of tennis, but Piquet's mind was on motorsports. When he was about 16 years old, Piquet started racing cars in his home country of Brazil. Piquet went off to college, but he left after a year to pursue a racing career.

FUN FACT

Formula racing has been a family affair for Nelson Piquet. His son Nelson Junior raced in Formula 1 in the 2008 and 2009 seasons, and his son Pedro raced in Formula 2.

Piquet races at the European Grand Prix.

In 1977, Piquet joined Formula 3, where he had a lot of success. By 1979, he was racing for Formula 1. In 1980, Piquet came in second place for the World Championship, but he took the title the following year. Piquet won again in 1983 and 1987.

By the early 1990s, Piquet had left Formula 1 and tried to qualify for the Indianapolis 500. A car accident left him with injuries before he was able to compete. Piquet raced for a few more years but later left racing to start a new company.

DRIVER STATS

- **Country**: Brazil
- **Years Raced in Formula 1**: 1978 to 1991
- **World Championship Wins**: 1981, 1983, 1987
- **Number of Formula 1 Wins**: 23

ALAIN PROST

Alain Prost grew up as an active kid, playing many sports, including wrestling, soccer, and even roller skating. But nothing caught his attention like racing. While on vacation with his family, Prost discovered go-kart racing for the first time. In 1974 at the age of 19, Prost began racing full-time. The following year, he won the French Senior Karting Championship before moving up to Formula 3 racing. He won the Formula 3 Championships in 1978 and 1979, solidifying himself as an up-and-coming driver. This success led to a deal with Formula 1 in 1980.

Prost's first season with F1 was a bit rocky with some accidents and minor injuries, but he won the 1981 French Grand Prix. In 1985, he won his first World

FUN FACT

Alain Prost was nicknamed "The Professor" because he has a serious and very detailed way of thinking about racing.

Prost celebrates a win at the Brazilian Grand Prix.

Prost drives a McLaren in the European Grand Prix.

Championship, becoming the first French racer to nab the title. The following year, Prost set another record: he won a second World Championship, becoming the first driver to win back-to-back championships since Jack Brabham 26 years before. He continued to beat old records and make new ones. In 1987, Prost won his 28th Grand Prix race, beating a 14-year record of 27 wins set by driver Jackie Stewart.

Though he did not take the 1988 Championship title, Prost earned it again in 1989 and 1993. He is one of only a few drivers that have won more than one World Championship.

DRIVER STATS

- **Country**: France
- **Years Raced in Formula 1**: 1980 to 1991; 1993
- **World Championship Wins**: 1985, 1986, 1989, 1993
- **Number of Formula 1 Wins**: 51

KIMI RAIKKONEN

Kimi Raikkonen raced motocross bikes with his brother at just three years old. By the time he was 10, Raikkonen was racing go-karts. Six years later, at 16, he decided to become a mechanic to continue his involvement in motorsports.

Raikkonen had a lot of success as a racer in his younger years. He eventually joined an entry-level racing event called Formula Renault and soon won two championships. He was asked to test drive for Formula 1. At the time, Raikkonen had driven only 23 professional races. In 2000, he was signed to Formula 1 at just 21 years old.

In 2003, three years into his Formula 1 career, Raikkonen came in second place in the World Championship. He came in second again in 2005, but in 2007, he took the top spot.

DRIVER STATS

- **Country**: Finland
- **Years Raced in Formula 1**: 2001 to 2009; 2012 to 2021
- **World Championship Wins**: 2007
- **Number of Formula 1 Wins**: 21

FUN FACT

Kimi Raikkonen was nicknamed the "Iceman" for his quiet demeanor.

JOCHEN RINDT

DRIVER STATS

- **Country**: Austria
- **Years Raced in Formula 1**: 1964 to 1970
- **World Championship Wins**: 1970
- **Number of Formula 1 Wins**: 6

Jochen Rindt had a passion for racing from a young age. He began with skiing, moped, and motorcycle racing. In the early 1960s, Rindt began racing cars. He was considered an aggressive driver. He was often in accidents. By 1964, Rindt bought a Formula 2 car. In his first race, he beat well-known Formula driver Graham Hill. None of the sports commentators knew who Rindt was at the time.

By 1965, Rindt had signed a Formula 1 contract and drove for a few different teams. In 1969, while driving for Team Lotus, he won his first championship race, the United States Grand Prix. The following year, while at a practice session in Italy, Rindt was killed in an accident. He was just 28 years old. Though he died before the end of the 1970 season, Jochen had the highest point total and was still awarded the 1970 World Championship title.

FUN FACT

A monument was built for Jochen Rindt at the Red Bull Ring in Spielberg, Austria. Turn number 9 on the track is also named after him.

Rindt holds up a trophy after winning an F2 race.

KEKE ROSBERG

As a teen, Keke Rosberg was a go-karting champion in Finland. In 1973, he became the Scandinavian and European go-kart champion too.

By 1975, Rosberg moved from go-karting up to the junior leagues of Formula racing. He single-handedly won almost half of the races in those series. His races kept him on the move: in 1978 alone, Rosberg competed in 41 competitions on five different continents.

For a few years after that, Rosberg did not have much racing success. But in 1980, he was asked to join a new team after fellow Formula 1 driver Alan Jones announced he would retire. It was an opportunity for Rosberg to prove himself again. Two years later, Rosberg won the F1 World Championship.

FUN FACT

Keke Rosberg drove for Finland, but he was born in Stockholm, Sweden.

DRIVER STATS

- **Country**: Finland
- **Years Raced in Formula 1**: 1978 to 1986
- **World Championship Wins**: 1982
- **Number of Formula 1 Wins**: 5

NICO ROSBERG

Nico Rosberg followed in his famous father's footsteps becoming a Formula 1 driver and World Champion. Rosberg started in go-karting when he was 10 years old and kept up with it as a teenager. He competed against Lewis Hamilton, who would later become his go-karting teammate.

By 2002, Rosberg left go-kart racing for car racing. In 2006, he was signed to race for Formula 1. He joined a few different teams over the years. He and Lewis Hamilton were reunited again in 2013 as teammates for the Mercedes team. In 2014 and 2015, Rosberg continued to win races, but he did not win the top prize. Finally in 2016, Rosberg became the World Champion.

DRIVER STATS

- **Country**: Germany
- **Years Raced in Formula 1**: 2006 to 2016
- **World Championship Wins**: 2016
- **Number of Formula 1 Wins**: 23

FUN FACT

Nico Rosberg's parents made sure he kept up with school while pursuing racing. In addition to being a good student, he learned to speak five languages.

JODY SCHECKTER

Jody Schekter's interest in racing started with motorcycles and soon moved to cars. At age 20 in 1970, he drove for the Formula Ford series and won the series that year.

Scheckter had a reputation for being wild behind the wheel. He often crashed his cars while driving in Formula Ford and Formula 3 races. Despite this, people could see his talent behind the wheel. In 1972, he began driving for Formula 1. Seven years later, Scheckter won the coveted World Championship.

DRIVER STATS

- **Country**: South Africa
- **Years Raced in Formula 1**: 1972 to 1980
- **World Championship Wins**: 1979
- **Number of Formula 1 Wins**: 10

AYRTON SENNA

Charming, smart, and lightning-fast is how Ayrton Senna was known on the track. His first taste of racing was in a go-kart at 13 years old. From there, Senna knew he wanted to become a race car driver. By 21, he was in Britain driving cars and winning races. Senna was just 24 years old when he made his Formula 1 debut in 1984. He came in second during his first race, which took place during a downpour of rain.

In 1988, Senna won his first World Championship by one race. His teammate Alain Prost came in second. Two years later, in 1990, Senna took the title again and repeated the feat the following year. Tragically, Senna was killed in an accident at the San Marino Grand Prix in 1994 during a race that was broadcast on television.

DRIVER STATS

- **Country:** Brazil
- **Years Raced in Formula 1:** 1984 to 1994
- **World Championship Wins:** 1988, 1990, 1991
- **Number of Formula 1 Wins:** 41

FUN FACT

The McLaren Senna is a sports car named after the famous driver Ayrton Senna.

Senna has been honored in his home country of Brazil and by many fans around the world.

MICHAEL SCHUMACHER

Michael Schumacher is considered one of the best Formula 1 drivers in the history of the sport. During his career, he broke record after record.

Schumacher was already winning championships as a child. When he was six, he won his first go-kart championship. By 18, he was the German and European go-kart champion. At that point, Schumacher decided to leave school to work as a car mechanic, which he did until he became a full-time race car driver. At 21, he became the Formula 3 German champion and made his Formula 1 debut the following year. During his first four years in Formula 1, Schumacher won 18 races and two World Championships in 1994 and 1995.

FUN FACT

Michael Schumacher earned seven World Championships. Lewis Hamilton is the only other F1 driver to have matched this record.

Schumacher races in a Ferrari.

Schumacher wins the Grand Prix of San Marino.

In 2000, Schumacher was racing for Team Ferrari and landed the team's first championship in more than 20 years. He broke Juan Manuel Fangio's record for the most World Championship titles, when he nabbed his sixth win in 2003. The following year, Schumacher won the World Championship again by a big margin. He won 13 of the 18 races that took place that year.

In December 2013, Schumacher was in a skiing accident in Switzerland. He suffered a massive brain injury. He has not raced since the accident.

DRIVER STATS

- **Country**: Germany
- **Years Raced in Formula 1**: 1991 to 2006; 2010 to 2012
- **World Championship Wins**: 1994, 1995, 2000, 2001, 2002, 2003, 2004
- **Number of Formula 1 Wins**: 91

JACKIE STEWART

Growing up in Scotland, Jackie Stewart spent a lot of time around cars. His father owned a car garage business, and his older brother Jimmy raced cars. Jackie wanted to do the same. At age 24, he entered Formula 3 and won seven races his first year. Two years later, in 1965, Stewart had reached racing's top tier: Formula 1.

Stewart won his first World Championship in 1969, then again in 1971 and 1973. After three major wins, he was becoming known as one of Formula's best-ever drivers. But it is what he accomplished off the track that may be even more

DRIVER STATS

- **Country**: United Kingdom
- **Years Raced in Formula 1**: 1965 to 1973
- **World Championship Wins**: 1969, 1971, 1973
- **Number of Formula 1 Wins**: 27

Stewart helped to improve helmets.

notable. Stewart had a mission to improve safety for all race car drivers.

Many drivers have lost their lives in Formula 1 racing. Stewart worked to make changes. He made sure that full-face helmets were required for all drivers. He also fought to require seat belts. Stewart helped to establish a traveling medical team that would be able to treat injuries on site at every race.

After his racing career ended, Stewart became a television sports commentator.

Stewart after racing at Silverstone Circuit

FORMULA 1: F.Y.I.

Formula 1 helmets include 17 layers of protection for drivers. The exterior layer is made from carbon fiber, which is tougher than the glass fiber used in years past. The shell, made of foam, helps absorb impact and distribute weight. The push foam layer is made from a softer material meant for comfort and a good fit. As part of the safety testing, a large steel anvil is dropped on the helmets from a height of about 11 feet (3 m).

JOHN SURTEES

John Surtees grew up in London where his father had a motorcycle repair shop and was a championship motorbike racer. Surtees followed in his father's footsteps, becoming a motorcycle engineer as well as a successful bike racer himself.

FUN FACT

John Surtees was the only F1 driver to have won World Championships in F1 car racing and in motorcycle racing.

By 25 years old, Surtees made the transition to racing cars, beginning with Formula 3. In 1960, he was signed by Team Lotus to race four Formula 1 events. He placed second in two of the four races. By 1963, Surtees signed on with Team Ferrari as their top driver. He won his first championship race at the German Grand Prix the same year.

In 1964, Surtees was crowned the Formula 1 World Champion. He continued racing for a number of years, and in 1969, he formed his own team: Team Surtees.

Surtees retired from driving in 1973 but kept on as a team owner. In 1978, he retired from Formula 1 as an owner.

DRIVER STATS

- **Country**: United Kingdom
- **Years Raced in Formula 1**: 1960 to 1972
- **World Championship Wins**: 1964
- **Number of Formula 1 Wins**: 6

Surtees at the Silverstone Circuit

MAX VERSTAPPEN

Max Verstappen was surrounded by racing as a kid. His mother was a winning go-kart racer, and his father drove for Formula 1. Verstappen started driving go-karts by the time he was four years old. As he got older, he continued to race go-karts and won numerous races.

In 2014, at 17 years old, Verstappen joined the Red Bull Junior racing team. Just one year later, he made his Formula 1 debut as part of the junior team. His first race was in Spain. He finished in fifth place, a solid race for a new, young driver. Though he did not win a race that year, Verstappen was named Rookie of the Year.

DRIVER STATS

- **Country**: Netherlands
- **Years Raced in Formula 1**: 2015 to present
- **World Championship Wins**: 2021, 2022, 2023
- **Number of Formula 1 Wins**: 54 (as of 2023)

Verstappen celebrates a win at the Dutch Grand Prix.

Verstappen competes for Red Bull Racing at the Yas Marina Circuit.

Verstappen was thought to be a somewhat reckless driver, but he continued to improve each year and began winning races. By 2019, he placed third in the World Championship, and he repeated his third-place position again in 2020, behind Lewis Hamilton and Valtteri Bottas.

COVID-19 changed racing schedules in 2021, but Formula 1 held 22 races that year. It was the same year the 24-year-old Max Verstappen won his first World Championship. He repeated his win in 2022. In 2023, he won his third Formula 1 World Championship. He was just 26 years old. Verstappen signed a contract to continue with Red Bull racing until 2028.

FUN FACT

Max Verstappen holds many records related to being the youngest driver in F1. He is the youngest points scorer, the youngest race starter, the youngest race leader, and the youngest fastest lap setter.

SEBASTIAN VETTEL

Growing up in Germany, Sebastian Vettel began racing go-karts when he was seven years old. He began winning races almost immediately. He was soon invited to join Red Bull's young driver training program, which helped cover the costs of car racing, a sport that can be expensive. By the time Vettel was 17, he had won 18 of the 20 races he entered. By 19, he was a test driver for F1's BMW Sauber team and made his Formula 1 debut at the

DRIVER STATS

- **Country**: Germany
- **Years Raced in Formula 1**: 2007 to 2022
- **World Championship Wins**: 2010, 2011, 2012, 2013
- **Number of Formula 1 Wins**: 53

Vettel drives an Aston Martin at the Italian Grand Prix.

United States Grand Prix in Indianapolis.

In 2009, Vettel joined Red Bull Racing and won the Formula 1 race in China, scoring the team's first F1 win. Vettel won his first Formula 1 World Championship in 2010, breaking the record as the youngest person to do so. He went on to take the win for the next three years.

FORMULA 1: F.Y.I.

Formula 1 is based on a point system. Points are awarded according to a driver's finishing place. But only the top 10 finishers are awarded points. The winner of a Grand Prix race receives 25 points; second place gets 18 points; third place gets 15 points. The points keep dropping, with the 10th position receiving one point. The driver who has the fastest lap gets an extra point as do teams that finish a race within the top 10. There are also points awarded during sprint races, which are short races with a distance of 62 miles (100 km). A Formula 1 World Championship title goes to the driver with the most points at the end of the season. This usually means that driver has also had the most first place finishes.

JACQUES VILLENEUVE

Jacques Villeneuve's father was an accomplished driver for Team Ferrari. Villeneuve watched his father race from the time he was just a toddler. In 1982, his father died while practicing for the Belgian Grand Prix. Villeneuve was sent to boarding school. It was there that he made the choice to become a race car driver.

Villeneuve joined Formula 3 racing in Europe and also raced in the United States. At 24 years old, he became the youngest winner of two major US races: the Indianapolis 500 and the IndyCar Championship. In 1996, at age 25, he joined Formula 1. Just one year later, he won seven F1 races to become one of the youngest World Championship winners.

DRIVER STATS

- **Country**: Canada
- **Years Raced in Formula 1**: 1996 to 2006
- **World Championship Wins**: 1997
- **Number of Formula 1 Wins**: 11

FORMULA 1: F.Y.I.

There are numerous fathers and sons and siblings who have become professional Formula 1 race car drivers, including Jacques Villeneuve, son of Gilles Villeneuve; Max Verstappen, son of Jos Verstappen; Nico Rosberg, son of Keke Rosberg; and Damon Hill, son of Graham Hill. The children of F1 drivers often have an advantage breaking into the sport. More so than their name, they have the guidance of a family member who has gone through the rigorous process. Often, they also have the financial means to join race car driving. Formula 1 is a sport that requires not only a big time commitment and plenty of dedication, but often a hefty financial commitment as well.

Villeneuve prepares to drive his late father's Ferrari.

F1 TEAMS AND DRIVERS

Formula 1 is made up of 10 teams. Each team has four drivers, but only two drivers participate in each race. Drivers on the same team drive the same car model. Teammates compete against each other and against the other F1 teams on the track.

The drivers are just two members of a much larger team. Each Formula 1 team is also made up of a team lead, a technical director who manages the development and building of the race car, and many other people who travel with each team to make sure each race runs smoothly.

Each team works hard to build cars that have the latest technology and the best aerodynamics to give them an advantage over other teams.

Sebastian Vettel and the Ferrari team get ready to race.

ALPINE

Alpine is one of the newer teams in Formula 1. It had its first F1 race in 2021. But the team has been around for many years. The team started off as Toleman Motorsport in 1981. Over the years, it has been known as several other names. Prior to being Alpine, the team was Renault Sport Formula 1 Team. Renault is a carmaker from France. Though Alpine is a French team, they are based in the United Kingdom.

Pierre Gasly

PIERRE GASLY

DRIVER STATS

- **Number**: 10
- **Country**: France
- **Grand Prix Entered**: 130
- **World Championships**: N/A
- **Date of Birth**: July 2, 1996

ESTEBAN OCON

DRIVER STATS

- **Number**: 31
- **Country**: France
- **Grand Prix Entered**: 133
- **World Championships**: N/A
- **Date of Birth**: September 17, 1996

Esteban Ocon

ASTON MARTIN
FORMULA ONE™ TEAM

ASTON MARTIN

Aston Martin is a car company that was founded in 1913 in London, England. The company began racing as a way to promote and sell their cars. Aston Martin's first Grand Prix was in 1922. Its first Formula 1 race was in 1959 but only raced in two F1 seasons. In the 2010s, Aston Martin returned to F1 as a sponsor and supplier to other teams. In 2021, Aston Martin formed their own team once again.

FERNANDO ALONSO

DRIVER STATS

- **Number**: 14
- **Country**: Spain
- **Grand Prix Entered**: 380
- **World Championships**: 2
- **Date of Birth**: July 29, 1981

Fernando Alonso

Lance Stroll

LANCE STROLL

DRIVER STATS

- **Number**: 18
- **Country**: Canada
- **Grand Prix Entered**: 143
- **World Championships**: N/A
- **Date of Birth**: October 29, 1998

FERRARI

Ferrari is an iconic Formula 1 team. They are also the most successful. They have won 16 World Constructors' titles and 15 driver World Championships. Ferrari has competed in every World Championship since 1950. In 2020, the team celebrated its 1,000th race at the Tuscan Grand Prix.

Charles Leclerc

CHARLES LECLERC

DRIVER STATS

- **Number**: 16
- **Country**: Monaco
- **Grand Prix Entered**: 125
- **World Championships**: N/A
- **Date of Birth**: October 16, 1997

CARLOS SAINZ JR.

DRIVER STATS

- **Number**: 55
- **Country**: Spain
- **Grand Prix Entered**: 185
- **World Championships**: N/A
- **Date of Birth**: September 1, 1994

Carlos Sainz Jr.

HAAS F1 TEAM

The Haas Formula 1 Team was founded in 2014 by Gene Haas, who began Haas Automation, one of the largest machine tool makers in the United States. Gene Haas also owns a NASCAR Sprint Cup Series team. Haas is headquartered in North Carolina. They also have a factory in the United Kingdom.

Haas had its debut race in 2016. As of 2023, it is the only American team in Formula 1 and the first American team in 30 years.

NICO HULKENBERG

DRIVER STATS

- **Number**: 27
- **Country**: Germany
- **Grand Prix Entered**: 206
- **World Championships**: N/A
- **Date of Birth**: August 19, 1987

Nico Hulkenberg

Kevin Magnussen

KEVIN MAGNUSSEN

DRIVER STATS

- **Number**: 20
- **Country**: Denmark
- **Grand Prix Entered**: 164
- **World Championships**: N/A
- **Date of Birth**: October 5, 1992

MCLAREN FORMULA 1 TEAM

Bruce McLaren Motor Racing was founded in 1963 by New Zealander Bruce McLaren. The McLaren team made their Formula 1 debut in 1966 at the Monaco Grand Prix. McLaren has had several legendary drivers including Emerson Fittipaldi, Niki Lauda, Alain Prost, and Ayrton Senna. Since its founding, McLaren has won 12 Formula 1 World Championships, 183 Formula 1 Grand Prix races, and 8 World Constructors' Championships.

Lando Norris

LANDO NORRIS

DRIVER STATS

- **Number**: 4
- **Country**: United Kingdom
- **Grand Prix Entered**: 104
- **World Championships**: N/A
- **Date of Birth**: November 13, 1999

Oscar Piastri

OSCAR PIASTRI

DRIVER STATS

- **Number**: 81
- **Country**: Australia
- **Grand Prix Entered**: 22
- **World Championships**: N/A
- **Date of Birth**: April 6, 2001

MERCEDES-AMG PETRONAS F1 TEAM

Mercedes-AMG Petronas F1 is a German team that is based in the United Kingdom. Mercedes competed in the early Grand Prix races in Europe during the 1930s. Its debut in Formula 1 was in 1954 at the French Grand Prix. In 1955, however, Mercedes left motor racing after a crash at the 24 Hours of Le Mans led to the deaths of more than 80 spectators and a driver. In 2010, Mercedes returned to F1 racing as a team once again. George Russell and Lewis Hamilton are the team's drivers. However, in 2025, Hamilton will move to the Ferrari team.

Lewis Hamilton

George Russell

LEWIS HAMILTON

DRIVER STATS

- **Number**: 44
- **Country**: United Kingdom
- **Grand Prix Entered**: 332
- **World Championships**: 7
- **Date of Birth**: January 7, 1985

GEORGE RUSSELL

DRIVER STATS

- **Number**: 63
- **Country**: United Kingdom
- **Grand Prix Entered**: 104
- **World Championships**: N/A
- **Date of Birth**: February 15, 1998

RED BULL RACING

Red Bull Racing debuted in 2005.
The team was founded by Dietrich Mateschitz, who owns the energy drink company with the same name. Mateschitz saw motorsports as a way to market his energy drinks.

Red Bull has had a lot of success since it began. The team has won six World Constructors' Championships and seven driver World Championships. Red Bull Racing has a second F1 team, Visa Cash App RB, where drivers practice before moving up the Red Bull team.

Sergio "Checo" Perez

SERGIO "CHECO" PEREZ

DRIVER STATS

- **Number**: 11
- **Country**: Mexico
- **Grand Prix Entered**: 258
- **World Championship**: N/A
- **Date of Birth**: January 26, 1990

MAX VERSTAPPEN

DRIVER STATS

- **Number**: 1
- **Country**: Netherlands
- **Grand Prix Entered**: 185
- **World Championships**: 3
- **Date of Birth**: September 30, 1997

Max Verstappen

STAKE F1 TEAM KICK SAUBER

Stake F1 Team Kick Sauber was formed in 2024, replacing Alfa Romeo after its 2023 season. The Swiss team will also have a brand-new car called the Kick Sauber C44. In 2026, Stake F1 Team Kick Sauber will change to team Audi.

For the next two years, the cars will be powered by Ferrari's engines. Once Audi fully takes over in 2026, the cars will be built with Audi engines and, like every year, be given a whole new look.

VALTTERI BOTTAS

Valtteri Bottas

DRIVER STATS

- **Number**: 77
- **Country**: Finland
- **Grand Prix Entered**: 222
- **World Championships**: N/A
- **Date of Birth**: August 28, 1989

Zhou Guanyu

ZHOU GUANYU

DRIVER STATS

- **Number**: 24
- **Country**: China
- **Grand Prix Entered**: 44
- **World Championships**: N/A
- **Date of Birth**: May 30, 1999

VISA CASH APP RB

Renamed in 2024 for its sponsors, the Visa Cash App RB was formed in 2006. The team was formerly known as AlphaTauri. The RB in the team's name stands for Red Bull. It was created as a spin-off of Red Bull racing to help launch the careers of young drivers.

DANIEL RICCIARDO

Daniel Ricciardo

DRIVER STATS

- **Number**: 3
- **Country**: Australia
- **Grand Prix Entered**: 239
- **World Championships**: N/A
- **Date of Birth**: January 7, 1989

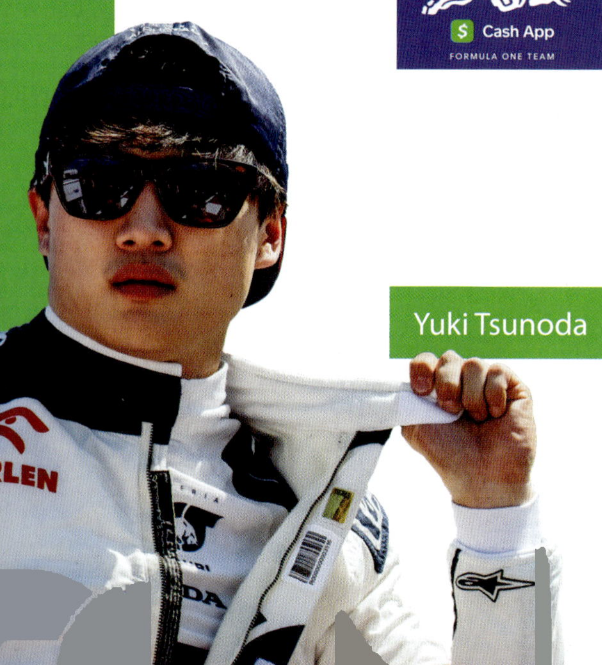
Yuki Tsunoda

YUKI TSUNODA

DRIVER STATS

- **Number**: 22
- **Country**: Japan
- **Grand Prix Entered**: 66
- **World Championships**: N/A
- **Date of Birth**: May 11, 2000

WILLIAMS RACING

The Williams Formula 1 team was founded in 1977 by Frank Williams, a race car driver and enthusiast from the United Kingdom. During the 1980s and 1990s, the team had many wins, but their successes dropped in the 2000s. The COVID-19 pandemic brought financial hardship to Williams. In 2020, Dorilton Capital, an American company, bought Williams Racing, but the team kept its name. In 2022, Alex Albon joined the team with a successful first year, bringing Williams Racing back into the spotlight.

Alexander Albon

ALEXANDER ALBON

WILLIAMS RACING

DRIVER STATS

- **Number**: 23
- **Country**: Thailand
- **Grand Prix Entered**: 81
- **World Championships**: N/A
- **Date of Birth**: March 23, 1996

LOGAN SARGEANT

Logan Sargeant

DRIVER STATS

- **Number**: 2
- **Country**: United States
- **Grand Prix Entered**: 22
- **World Championships**: N/A
- **Date of Birth**: December 31, 2000

F2 AND F3 TEAMS

ART GRAND PRIX

The French motor company ART Grand Prix was founded in 1996 under the name ASM F3. The team started racing in Formula 3 that same year. In 2004, the team was renamed ART Grand Prix, and the following year, it made its debut in the Formula 2 series. ART has helped develop some of Formula 1's top drivers, including Lewis Hamilton, Charles Leclerc, Sebastian Vettel, Nico Rosberg, and George Russell.

Many teams, including ART Grand Prix, race in both F2 and F3 races. ART Grand Prix was undefeated in the Formula 3 Euro Series between 2004 and 2009. The team earned a total of 51 wins in that time. In 2022, ART driver Victor Martins secured the F3 World Championship.

Nikola Tsolov competes for ART Grand Prix.

CAMPOS RACING

It's been 26 years since Campos Racing first took to the track under the name Campos Motorsports. Based in Spain, the team was founded by a former Formula 1 driver named Adrián Campos. In its early years, Campos Motorsports was competing in numerous European racing series. By 2005, the team changed its name to Campos Racing and entered the GP2, a Formula series that was a feeder into Formula 1. The team continued to compete successfully in GP2 and Formula 2. Campos also competes in Formula 3.

FUN FACT

Each Formula series is allocated a certain number of tires per race. In F3, each driver gets four sets of tires for dry weather and two sets of tires for wet weather per race.

DAMS

Driot *Associés* Motor Sports, DAMS for short, is a French team that was founded in 1998 by Jean-Paul Driot and former F1 driver René Arnoux. DAMS competed in Formula 3000, a series that fed into Formula 1 racing, and later in GP2, which replaced Formula 3000. During its time in Formula 3000, DAMS had 21 wins and 4 team and 3 driver titles, making it one of the most successful teams in the series. The team has been competing in Formula 2 since 2017. More than 33 former DAMS drivers have gone on to Formula 1 racing, including Pierre Gasly, Kevin Magnussen, and Alexander Albon.

FUN FACT

In addition to F2 racing, DAMS has also competed in the 24 Hours of Le Mans and the Formula E Championship.

Ayumu Iwasa driving for DAMS

HITECH PULSE-EIGHT

Hitech Pulse-Eight is based in the United Kingdom, more specifically in Silverstone, England, near the famous Silverstone Circuit.

The British team was founded in 2002. It started in Formula 3 and the South American F3 series, Formula 3 Sudamericana. The team was originally known as Hitech Racing, but "Pulse-Eight" was added to the team's name in 2023. Pulse-Eight manufactures audio and video products and sponsors the team. The organization participates in F2, F3, and Formula 4, which is a junior category racing series that helps young drivers bridge the gap between go-kart racing and formula racing.

Luke Browning races in F3.

Jak Crawford at the Australian Grand Prix

Jak Crawford racing for Hitech Pulse-Eight

INVICTA VIRTUOSI RACING

Invicta Virtuosi Racing is a British team that formed in 2012. It started in Auto GP, a European racing series that ran from 1999 to 2016. After Auto GP, Invicta moved on to the GPF2, a former junior Formula series. In 2014, Invicta took over the Russian Time team, bringing it into Invicta Virtuosi Racing. In 2017, the team won the Formula 2 Championship. In addition to competing in Formula 2, Invicta also participates in the British Formula 4 series.

Jack Doohan competing for Invicta Virtuosi Racing

JENZER MOTORSPORT

Jenzer Motorsport was founded in 1993 by Andreas Jenzer, a racing driver. The team is based in Switzerland. Jenzer competes in Formula 3 and in Formula 4, but it does not compete in Formula 2. Many drivers, including Yuki Tsunoda and Oscar Piastri, have moved up the Formula ranks to F1 from the Jenzer F3 team.

MP MOTORSPORT

MP Motorsport is a Dutch team that was founded in 1995. It races in F1, F2, F3, and F4, and in racing series outside Formula 1. Their drivers come from more than 20 different countries. In 2022, MP won both the F2 driver and team championships. Today, MP Motorsport participates in more than 50 races all over the world, including Formula 2.

In 2019, Richard Verschoor, driving for MP Motorsport, won the F3 Macau Grand Prix. The street race, held in Macau, China, made its debut in 1954. While there are several car and motorcycle races over the course of the Macau Grand Prix race weekend, the F3 race is considered the most important. Its winner often becomes the F3 World Champion.

Franco Colapinto competes for MP Motorsport.

PHM RACING

PHM Racing races in F2, F3, and F4. The German team is new to the racing world. It was established in 2021 as a nonprofit organization. The team's goal is to help young drivers enter motorsports without having to worry about the high cost of professional racing. The team does this in part through government assistance in the form of grants, money that is given without the obligation to pay it back. Among other things, PHM uses the money to train drivers all year, during and after the racing season.

PREMA RACING

Prema Racing was founded in 1983. It is one of the larger teams in the Formula world and third largest in Italian motorsports. Over the years, Prema has won multiple championships, including 2020 and 2021 team and driver championships. Prema is made up of more than 60 members who work to develop a new generation of drivers in F2, F3, and F4.

In 2019, the first Formula 3 World Championship was held. Prema Racing has had more F3 winners than any other team. As of 2023, Prema has won the team championship four of the five years, with Trident being the only other winning team with a victory in 2021.

Oliver Bearman drives for Prema Racing.

Oliver Gray of Rodin Motorsport drives in the pit lane.

RODIN MOTORSPORT

Rodin Motorsport, a British racing team, has had more than 400 victories since it was founded in the late 1990s. Rodin Motorsport competes in several types of races including F2, F3, and F4 races. In 2023, they also joined the Spanish F4, and F1 Academy, Formula's all-female racing series.

Rodin Motorsport was the first team to join a new type of racing series, the eSkootr Championship. ESkootr debuted in 2022. It is the first racing series of its kind. Riders race high-speed electric scooters on city streets.

ESkootr

TRIDENT MOTORSPORT

Based in Italy, Trident Motorsport made its debut in 2006, first at the GP2, which was Europe's second tier of racing behind Formula 1. GP2 is now known as Formula 2. Trident was founded by Maurizio Salvadori, who has a background in show business. The Trident team strives to push the boundaries of technology and performance while also encouraging the personal and professional growth of its young drivers.

In 2023, Trident driver Gabriel Bortoleto was the F3 World Champion. This was the first F3 World Championship win for the Trident team. Bortoleto also won the Aramco Best Rookie Award the same year.

FUN FACT

The Trident factory in Milan, Italy, includes a room with a car simulator and a floor to ceiling screen. Drivers use the simulator to get comfortable with the cars and to practice maneuvers on the track.

Max Verstappen drives for Van Amersfoort during a Formula 3 race.

VAN AMERSFOORT RACING

Van Amersfoort Racing was founded in the Netherlands in 1975 by Frits van Amersfoort. VAR participates in F2, F3, and F4 races. They also compete in FRECA, which is a European racing series. They are committed to helping young drivers build their careers in auto racing. Their motto is "Passion. Dedication. Tradition."

At 16 years old, Formula 1 star driver Max Verstappen drove as a member of Van Amersfoort Racing's F3 team. He won six consecutive victories and ranked third overall in the F3 series.

F2 AND F3 DRIVERS

ANDREA KIMI ANTONELLI

DRIVER STATS

- **2024 Team:** Prema Racing
- **Number:** 4
- **Country:** Italy
- **Date of Birth:** August 25, 2006

Andrea Kimi Antonelli

Paul Aron

PAUL ARON

DRIVER STATS

- **2024 Team:** Hitech Pulse-Eight
- **Number:** 17
- **Country:** Estonia
- **Date of Birth:** February 04, 2004

OLIVER BEARMAN

DRIVER STATS

- **2024 Team:** Prema Racing
- **Number:** 3
- **Country:** United Kingdom
- **Date of Birth:** May 8, 2005

DINO BEGANOVIC

DRIVER STATS

- **2024 Team:** Prema Racing
- **Number:** 1
- **Country:** Sweden
- **Date of Birth:** January 19, 2004

Oliver Bearman

FUN FACT

In 2024, Oliver Bearman stepped in for Carlos Sainz Jr., who had appendicitis, and drove for Ferrari at the Saudi Arabian Grand Prix.

Dino Beganovic

GABRIEL BORTOLETO

Gabriel Bortoleto

DRIVER STATS

- **2024 Team:** Invicta Virtuosi Racing
- **Number:** 10
- **Country:** Brazil
- **Date of Birth:** October 14, 2004

FUN FACT

Gabriel Bortoleto was the 2023 F3 driver champion.

LUKE BROWNING

Luke Browning

DRIVER STATS

- **2024 Team:** Hitech Pulse-Eight
- **Number:** 14
- **Country:** United Kingdom
- **Date of Birth:** January 31, 2002

Franco Colapinto

FRANCO COLAPINTO

DRIVER STATS

- **2024 Team:** MP Motorsport
- **Number:** 12
- **Country:** Argentina
- **Date of Birth:** May 27, 2003

Amaury Cordeel

AMAURY CORDEEL

DRIVER STATS

- **2024 Team**: Hitech Pulse-Eight
- **Number**: 16
- **Country**: Belgium
- **Date of Birth**: July 9, 2002

FUN FACT

Juan Manuel Correa started racing motocross in Ecuador before getting into go-kart racing.

JUAN MANUEL CORREA

DRIVER STATS

- **2024 Team**: DAMS
- **Number**: 8
- **Country**: United States
- **Date of Birth**: August 09, 1999

Juan Manuel Correa

JAK CRAWFORD

DRIVER STATS

- **2024 Team**: DAMS
- **Number**: 7
- **Country**: United States
- **Date of Birth**: May 2, 2005

Jak Crawford

Enzo Fittipaldi

ENZO FITTIPALDI

DRIVER STATS

- **2024 Team**: Van Amersfoort Racing
- **Number**: 14
- **Country**: Brazil
- **Date of Birth**: July 18, 2001

FUN FACT

Sophia Floersch is the only woman in all of Formula 1, 2, or 3 racing. At 14 years old, she became the youngest to win the Ginetta Junior Championship, a racing series based in the United Kingdom. In 2023, she became the first woman to score points in Formula 3.

SOPHIA FLOERSCH

DRIVER STATS

- **2024 Team**: Van Amersfoort Racing
- **Number**: 21
- **Country**: Germany
- **Date of Birth**: December 1, 2000

Sophia Floersch

ISACK HADJAR

Isack Hadjar

DRIVER STATS

- **2024 Team:** Campos Racing
- **Number:** 20
- **Country:** France
- **Date of Birth:** September 28, 2004

DENNIS HAUGER

Dennis Hauger

DRIVER STATS

- **2024 Team:** MP Motorsport
- **Number:** 11
- **Country:** Norway
- **Date of Birth:** March 17, 2003

FUN FACT

Dennis Hauger's father, a rally car racer, served as Hauger's mechanic until he started racing in Italy.

Kush Maini

KUSH MAINI

DRIVER STATS

- **2024 Team:** Invicta Virtuosi Racing
- **Number:** 9
- **Country:** India
- **Date of Birth:** September 22, 2000

ZANE MALONEY

Zane Maloney

DRIVER STATS

- **2024 Team**: Rodin Motorsport
- **Number**: 5
- **Country**: Barbados
- **Date of Birth**: October 02, 2003

Christian Mansell

CHRISTIAN MANSELL

DRIVER STATS

- **2024 Team**: ART Grand Prix
- **Number**: 23
- **Country**: Australia
- **Date of Birth**: February 09, 2005

FUN FACT

In 2019, Christian Mansell was diagnosed with type 1 diabetes. But that has not stopped him from pursuing his racing career.

JOSEP MARÍA MARTÍ

DRIVER STATS

- **2024 Team**: Campos Racing
- **Number**: 21
- **Country**: Spain
- **Date of Birth**: June 13, 2005

Josep María Martí

Victor Martins

VICTOR MARTINS

DRIVER STATS

- **2024 Team**: ART Grand Prix
- **Number**: 1
- **Country**: France
- **Date of Birth**: June 16, 2001

GABRIELE MINÌ

DRIVER STATS

- **2024 Team**: Prema Racing
- **Number**: 2
- **Country**: Italy
- **Date of Birth**: March 20, 2005

Gabriele Minì

RITOMO MIYATA

DRIVER STATS

- **2024 Team:** Rodin Motorsport
- **Number:** 6
- **Country:** Japan
- **Date of Birth:** August 10, 1999

Ritomo Miyata

ZAK O'SULLIVAN

DRIVER STATS

- **2024 Team:** ART Grand Prix
- **Number:** 2
- **Country:** United Kingdom
- **Date of Birth:** February 06, 2005

Zak O'Sullivan

RICHARD VERSCHOOR

DRIVER STATS

- **2024 Team:** Trident
- **Number:** 22
- **Country:** Netherlands
- **Date of Birth:** December 16, 2000

Richard Verschoor

SPECIAL RULES

Racing and other sports have many rules and regulations that must be followed. Most are for safety. Formula 1 has some of the strictest rules in any sport.

To compete in Formula 1, drivers need to be at least 18 years old, have solid racing experience, and hold a special driver's license called a Super License.

Cars and drivers must meet a minimum weight requirement as their combined weight can affect the car's performance. All Formula 1 cars are required to weigh at least 1,759 pounds (798 kg). All drivers are weighed before a race. They must be at least 176 pounds (80 kg), including their gear. If the combined weight of the driver and the car is not enough, weights are added to the car.

Drivers are also weighed after a race. During a race, they can lose between 4 and 8 pounds (2 and 4 kg). Temperatures inside a race car can reach 122 degrees Fahrenheit (50 degrees

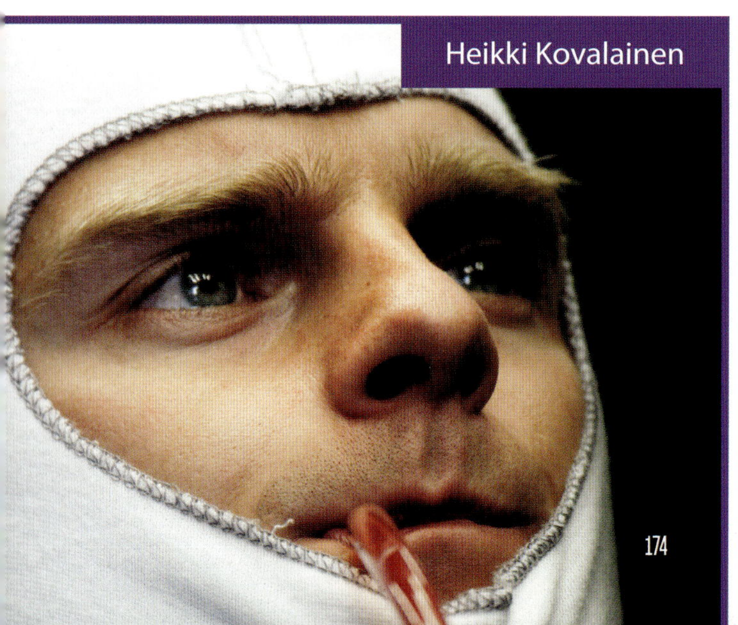

Heikki Kovalainen

FORMULA 1: F.Y.I.

Formula 1 cars have built-in drink stations. Drivers have a straw near their mouths that they can easily reach to have a drink during a race.

Celsius). This can cause drivers to sweat a lot, which results in weight loss. If drivers lose too much weight after a race, they will receive medical care to make sure their health is not affected by the weight loss.

Drivers must pick a driver number when they begin their careers, and they are required to keep the same number. The only time drivers can change their racing numbers is if they win the World Championship. The World Champion becomes number one while they hold the title.

Lewis Hamilton stops at the weigh bridge before a race.

PIT STOPS

A Formula 1 pit stop is a meticulously orchestrated and lightning-fast operation that can make or break a race. It involves a highly trained pit crew, a range of specialized tools, and precise choreography.

FUN FACT

Refueling during F1 races was banned in 2010 after multiple incidents of fires during refueling stops caused safety concerns.

TIRE CHANGERS
work as a team of four to quickly remove the old tires and replace them with new ones

TIRE CARRIERS
transport tires to and from the car

JACK OPERATORS
use high-speed jacks to lift the car off the ground to allow the tire changers to work swiftly

WHEEL OFF AND WHEEL ON TEAMS
remove and replace the car's wheels in a matter of seconds

WING ADJUSTERS
adjust the car's front and rear wings to maximize aerodynamics

LOLLIPOP MAN
uses a lollipop-shaped sign to tell the driver when it's time to leave the pit box

DATA ENGINEERS AND MECHANICS
monitor the car's performance and address engine or maintenance issues

PIT CREW CHIEF
coordinates the timing of pit stops and oversees the entire operation

FORMULA E

Formula E is a special branch of car racing for electric cars. The "E" in the name means "electric." Running fully on electricity makes Formula E cars sustainable.

The idea for Formula E came about in 2011 when a Spanish businessman and the president of the FIA discussed the idea of racing electric cars. Three years later in 2014, Formula E hosted its first race at the Olympic Park in Beijing, China.

FORMULA 1: F.Y.I.

The makers of Formula E cars share their technology with the makers of regular street cars in an attempt to help improve the electric cars on the roads.

Formula E pit stop

Formula E has 11 teams, 22 drivers, and 16 races per year. The races are 33 laps, and cars drive at speeds of up to 200 miles per hour (322 kmh). Instead of being called Grand Prix, these races are called E-Prix events. And like Formula 1 races, Formula E races take place all over the world.

The charge in the electric batteries used in FE cars are advanced enough to last the entire race. Drivers do not need to drive into the pit stop to recharge.

FUN FACT

Formula E drivers usually race on streets in the middle of major cities such as London and Tokyo.

London E-Prix

F1 ACADEMY

In 2023, the Formula 1 organization launched a new program called the F1 Academy, a new category of F1 racing for women. The goal of the F1 Academy is to promote, encourage, and prepare young female drivers for higher levels of F1 racing.

Many drivers, both male and female, get their start in racing at a young age through junior-level races such as go-karting. But there have been many fewer opportunities for girls and women in racing than for boys and men. The F1 Academy has created programs for girls to get involved in youth motorsports to build their interest in racing before joining the academy.

Once at the academy, female drivers can join one of the five F1 Academy teams. These teams are run by existing F2 and F3 teams. Each team has three drivers for a total of 15 female drivers. In 2023, there were 21 F1 Academy races that took place.

FORMULA 1: F.Y.I.

In addition to the F1 Academy, Formula 1 has created other programs to promote diversity. In 2019, the organization started a sustainability and diversity and inclusion program. One goal of the program is to bring in a more diverse group of drivers to help break stereotypes about what motorsports drivers look like.

Susie Wolff, Managing Director of F1 Academy, poses with drivers.

Lewis Hamilton with F1 Academy drivers at the Circuit of the Americas

FLAGS

When drivers are on the track, focusing on the road is not the only thing they need to do. They also need to pay attention to the flags being flown as they speed by. These racing flags provide important information to drivers, from signaling the first and last laps and notifying drivers of a disqualification to alerting them about debris or other problems on the track.

When a driver "takes the checkered flag," it means he or she has won the race.

BLACK
Driver is disqualified.

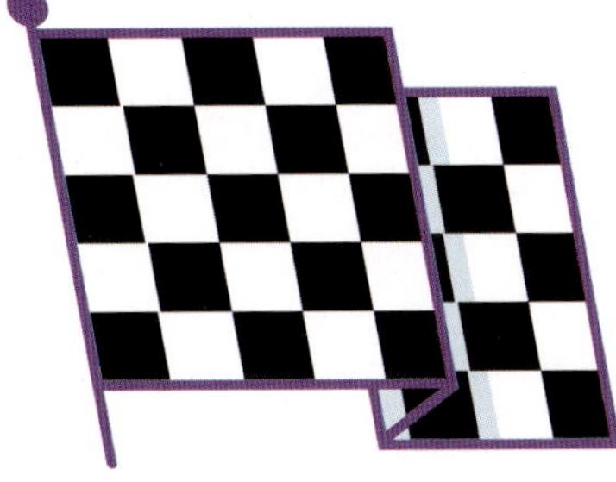

BLACK-AND-WHITE CHECKERED
The race has ended.

YELLOW
No overtaking, there is a hazard on the track.

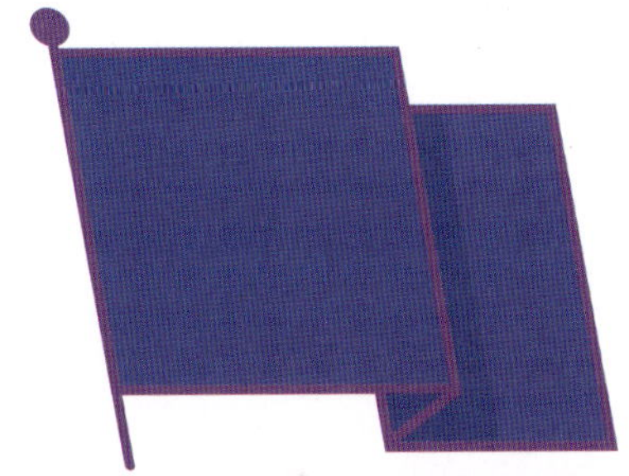

BLUE
Driver must move to the side to allow a faster driver to overtake them.

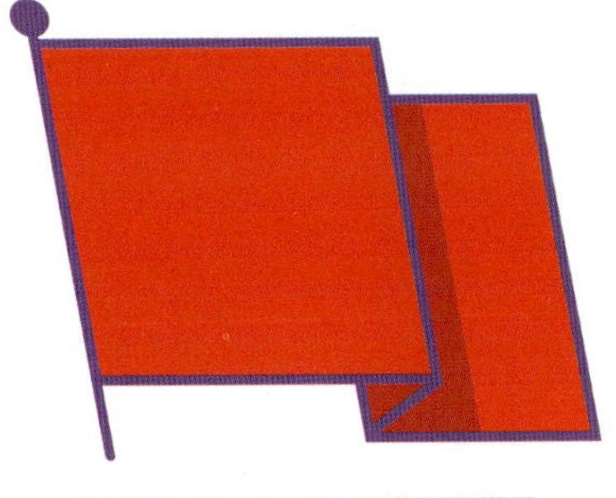

RED
Race is suspended.

GREEN
Full-speed racing is approved.

WORLD CONSTRUCTORS' CHAMPIONSHIP

Formula 1's World Constructors' Championship is an award given to the best carmaker each racing season. The winner is chosen based on points scored by drivers in races throughout the season. Points for every driver of each carmaker are added together. For example, if there are three Ferraris in an F1 race, the points earned by each of the three drivers will be added together to go toward the Constructors' title. At the end of the season, the carmaker with the most points wins the title of World Constructors' Champion.

The winner of the World Constructors' Champion not only gets a trophy, but the team also gets the largest cash prize of the top 10 teams—about $140 million. Second through tenth place also win money ranging from about $131 million for second place to $60 million for tenth place.

FERRARI

WILLIAMS

MCLAREN, MERCEDES

LOTUS

RED BULL RACING

BRABHAM, COOPER, RENAULT

BENETTON, BRAWN GP, BRM, MATRA, TYRELL, VANWALL

WINS BY CARMAKER

16

9

8

7

6

2

1

AFTER THE SEASON

Every Formula 1 car is designed and built to race for just one season. When a season is over, most of the cars go back to the factory where they were built to be deconstructed. All parts of the car are removed, except the chassis. The parts might be used to help develop new designs for future seasons, or they might be displayed somewhere such as in a museum. Engines are usually borrowed and must be returned to the manufacturer who built them. Sometimes, other car parts are borrowed and returned at the end of a season as well.

Some cars and car parts go into storage. Team McLaren has more than 50 retired cars in its top-secret storage facility known as Unit 2. There have also been a few cases of F1 teams gifting a car to a championship driver. Some cars are used in testing for junior drivers. In this case, an F1 race car must have been retired for at least two years to make sure all junior drivers are on equal footing.

Retired F1 cars are also used for demonstrations or at special racing events such as festivals. In some cases, the cars are sold to individual people who are interested in owning one.

In 2023, Lewis Hamilton's Mercedes F1 W04 race car, which he drove during the 2013 season, sold for almost $19 million.

FUN FACT

The 2023 Formula 1 season was nine months long. The first race was held in March in the country of Bahrain. The last race was held in Abu Dhabi, United Arab Emirates, in November.

GLOSSARY

aerodynamics
The way air moves around an object.

altitude
The vertical distance of an object above sea level.

artificial
Humanmade; not made by nature.

chassis
The supporting frame of a car.

displaced
Removed from its proper place.

downforce
A force of air that helps "press" a vehicle down on the road or track.

drag racing
A race between two cars over a short distance.

fuel economy
The distance a vehicle can travel on a specific amount of fuel.

horsepower
A measurement of power that a car engine produces.

overtake
In car racing, to catch up to something from behind, then pass it.

rigorous
Strict and demanding; something that takes a lot of detail and attention to accomplish.

rivalry
A competition for the same goal.

stereotype
An image or idea that society places on groups of people that is unfair or untrue.

sustainable
Able to be maintained or continued at a certain level.

TO LEARN MORE

FURTHER READING

Johnson, Bernadette. *Formula 1 Trivia Book*. Ulysses Press, September 2024. (Distributed by Simon and Schuster)

Mugford, Simon. *Sports Superstars: Lewis Hamilton Rules*. Welbeck Children's, May 2022.

Rule, Heather. *Formula One Racing Cars*. ABDO, August 2023.

ONLINE RESOURCES

To learn more about Formula 1, please visit **abdobooklinks.com** or scan this QR code. These links are routinely monitored and updated to provide the most current information available.

INDEX

PHOTO CREDITS

Cover Photos: S.Candide/Shutterstock, front (retro red race car); Clive Rose/Getty Images Sport/Getty Images, front (World Constructors' Championship trophy); VideoBCN/Shutterstock (Pirelli tire); cristiano barni/Shutterstock, front (rows of F1 cars), front (Michael Schumacher's Ferrari race car), front (Max Verstappen); majorstockphoto/Shutterstock, front (Ferrari flag); AlessioDeMarco/Shutterstock, front (Lewis Hamilton's Mercedes race car); mikeledray/Shutterstock, front (orange smoke); Michael Potts F1/Shutterstock, front (Max Verstappen's Red Bull Racing race car); Dan74/Shutterstock, back (#4 race car); Jens Mommens/Shutterstock, back (#16 race car)
Interior Photos: tcharts/Shutterstock, 1 (left); FiledIMAGE/Shutterstock, 1 (right), 23, 86 (top), 90, 91 (top), 155 (bottom), 156; David Ramos/Getty Images Sport/Getty Images, 2–3; Cliche Panajou/Les Sports modernes/Wikimedia Commons, 4; Library of Congress, Prints & Photographs Division, LC-DIG-ggbain-00117/Library of Congress, 5; Klemantaski Collection/Hulton Archive/Getty Images, 6, 10 (bottom); Central Press/Hulton Archive/Getty Images, 7 (top), 133; S.Candide/Shutterstock, 7 (bottom); Jakub Porzycki/NurPhoto/Getty Images, 8, 164 (right); AFP/Getty Images, 9 (top); Pascal Rondeau/ALLSPORT/ Getty Images Sport/Getty Images, 9 (bottom); OFF/AFP/Getty Images, 10 (top); Tony Duffy/Getty Images Sport/Getty Images, 11 (top left); Gregory Reed/Shutterstock, 11 (top right); Pascal Rondeau/Getty Images Sport/Getty Images, 11 (bottom); motorsports Photographer/Shutterstock, 12–13, 21, 27, 29, 32, 46, 47, 50, 51, 52, 54, 56, 57, 58, 60 (bottom), 82–83, 98, 135, 141 (bottom left), 142 (bottom), 143 (bottom), 145 (middle), 146 (bottom), 147 (bottom), 148 (middle), 149 (middle), 149 (bottom), 170 (middle), 185 (bottom); Aleksfoto/Shutterstock, 14–15; ATTILA KISBENEDEK/AFP/Getty Images, 16; Abdul Razak Latif/Shutterstock, 17 (top), 140, 176–177; Dan Istitene/Formula 1/Getty Images, 17 (bottom); Clari Massimiliano/Shutterstock, 20; Wirestock Creators/Shutterstock, 22; Jean-Philippe Navarro/Shutterstock, 24; Vanessa Machelett/Wikimedia Commons, 25; Jay Hirano Photography/Shutterstock, 26, 33, 39, 49, 141 (top), 150 (bottom), 151 (bottom); Sunil Onamkulam/Shutterstock, 28; Alex Pantling/Formula 1/Getty Images, 30, 168 (bottom), 171 (top); Jens Mommens/Shutterstock, 31; PatrickLauzon photographe/Shutterstock, 34, 137; Firefighter Montreal/Shutterstock, 35; Clive Mason/Getty Images Sports/Getty Images, 36; Charles Coates/Getty Images Sports/Getty Images, 37; MPPhotograph/Shutterstock, 38; ANP/Getty Images Sport/Getty Images, 40; PriceM/Shutterstock, 41 (top); cristiano barni/Shutterstock, 41 (bottom), 42, 44, 48, 55, 60 (top), 64, 65, 87, 88 (bottom), 91 (bottom), 108, 109,128, 129, 134, 136, 142 (middle), 144 (middle), 144 (bottom), 147 (top), 148 (bottom); Kurka Geza Corey/Shutterstock, 43; xbrchx/Shutterstock, 45; YES Market Media/Shutterstock, 53; pauloalberto82/Shutterstock, 59; Erphan Rahat/Shutterstock, 61; Michael Potts/BSR Agency/Getty Images Sport/Getty Images, 62; AhLamb/iStock Unreleased/Getty Images, 63; Grindstone Media Group/Shutterstock, 66; Jeff Schultes/Shutterstock, 67; Ryan Pierse/Getty Images Sport/Getty Images, 68, 69; Rudy Carezzevoli/Formula 1/Getty Images, 70–71, 161 (top), 165 (bottom), 166 (middle); Hulton Archive/Getty Images, 72; Dan74/Shutterstock, 73; Lothar Spurzem/Wikimedia Commons, 74; Joost Evers/Anefo/Dutch National Archives/Wikimedia Commons, 75; Takayuki Suzuki/Flickr, 76–77; Andrew Hone/Getty Images Sport/Getty Images, 77, 79; Evening Standard/Hulton Archive/Getty Images, 78, 104, 105, 130; Pascal Rondeau/Allsport/Hulton Archive/Getty Images, 80; Thesupermat/Wikimedia Commons, 81; Lukas Raich/Wikimedia Commons, 84, 85; Jared C. Tilton/Getty Images Sport/Getty Images, 86 (bottom); Mark Thompson/Getty Images Sport/Getty Images, 88 (top), 151 (middle left); AlessioDeMarco/Shutterstock, 89, 185 (top right); Guido De Bortoli/Formula 1/Getty Images, 92; samurai R photography/Shutterstock, 93; GP Library/Universal Images Group/Getty Images, 94 (top); Hans van Dijk/Anefo/Dutch National Archives/Wikimedia Commons, 94 (bottom); Bernard Cahier/Hulton Archive/Getty Images, 95; Express/Hulton Archive/Getty Images, 96, 107, 111, 114; Allsport/Hulton Archive/Getty Images, 97; Nufa Qaiesz/Shutterstock, 99; katacarix/Shutterstock, 100–101; spatuletail/Shutterstock, 101; ullstein bild/Getty Images, 102; Keystone/Hulton Archive/Getty Images, 103, 112, 126; Andreas Rentz/Bongarts/Getty Images, 106; Michael Cooper/Allsport/Hulton Archive/Getty Images, 110; Trevor Humphries/Hulton Archive/Getty Images, 113; Steve Powell/Allsport/Getty Images Sport/Getty Images, 115; McCarthy/Hulton Archive/Getty Images, 116; Mike Hewitt/Allsport/Hulton Archive/Getty Images, 117; Mike Powell/Getty Images Sport/Getty Images, 118; Mike Powell/Allsport/Getty Images Sport/Getty Images, 119; Simon Bruty/Allsport/Hulton Archive/Getty Images, 120; Mike King/Getty Images Sport/Getty Images, 121; Logan Riely/Getty Images Sport/Getty Images, 122; Victor Blackman/Hulton Archive/Getty Images, 123; Allsport/Getty Images Sport/Getty Images, 124; Formula E/Handout/Getty Images Sport/Getty Images, 125; Sutton/Getty Images Sport/Getty Images, 127; Wesley/Hulton Archive/Getty Images, 131; Roger Jackson/Hulton Archive/Getty Images, 132; Mike Cooper/Allsport/Getty images Sport/Getty Images, 138; Dan Istitene/Getty Images Sport/Getty Images, 139; Yshevchuk0206/Dreamstime.com, 141 (bottom right), 142 (top), 143 (top), 145 (top), 146 (top), 148 (top); Kym Illman/Getty Images Sport/Getty Images, 143 (top); Haas F1 Team/Wikimedia Commons, 144 (top); Qian Jun/MB Media/Getty Images Sport/Getty Images, 145 (bottom); KarlMarx1889/Wikimedia Commons, 149 (top); KaktusAAAA/Wikimedia Commons, 150 (middle left); sbonsi/Shutterstock, 150 (middle right); Microstock77/Dreamstime.com, 151 (middle right); Emmanuele Ciancaglini/Formula 1/Getty Images, 152, 172 (bottom); Andrea Bacuzzi/Dreamstime.com, 153; Bryn Lennon/Formula 1/Getty Images, 154, 163, 166 (bottom); Joe Portlock/Formula 1/Getty Images, 155 (top), 158, 159, 160, 164 (left), 166 (top), 167 (top), 168 (top), 170 (bottom), 171 (bottom), 172 (top), 173 (middle); Morgan Hancock/NurPhoto/Getty Images, 155 (middle); PHOTOMDP/Shutterstock, 157; Valerio Pennicino/Getty Images Sport/Getty Images, 161 (bottom); Darrell Ingham/Getty Images Sport/Getty Images, 162; Alex Pantling/Getty Images Sport/Getty Images, 165 (top); Kristin Greenwood/Shutterstock, 167 (bottom); Ker Robertson/Getty Images Sport/Getty Images, 169; Rudy Carezzevoli/Getty Images Sport/Getty Images, 170 (top), 173 (bottom); Clive Rose/Getty Images Sport/Getty Images, 172 (middle), 182, 185 (middle); James Gilbert/Getty Images Sport/Getty Images, 173 (top); Darren Heath Photographer/Hulton Archive/Getty Images, 174; Albert Gea/Pool/Getty Images Sport/Getty Images, 175; joharhu/Shutterstock, 176; Marco Iacobucci/Dreamstime.com, 178; Warren Little/Getty Images Sport/Getty Images, 179; Adam Pretty/Formula 1/Getty Images, 180; Jared C. Tilton/Formula 1/Getty Images, 181; Natursports/Shutterstock, 184; Kosarev Alexander/Shutterstock, 185 (top left); ZRyzner/Shutterstock, 186–187

ABDOBOOKS.COM

Published by Abdo Reference, a division of ABDO, PO Box 398166, Minneapolis, Minnesota 55439.

Printed in China
092024
012025

Editor: Carrie Hasler
Series Designer: Colleen McLaren

LIBRARY OF CONGRESS CONTROL NUMBER: 2023949520

PUBLISHER'S CATALOGING-IN-PUBLICATION DATA

Names: Lamichhane, Priyanka, author.
Title: The formula 1 encyclopedia / by Priyanka Lamichhane
Description: Minneapolis, Minnesota : Abdo Reference, 2025 | Series: Motorsports encyclopedias | Includes online resources and index.
Identifiers: ISBN 9781098294410 (lib. bdg.) | ISBN 9798384913689 (ebook)
Subjects: LCSH: Motorsports--Juvenile literature. | Motor racing--Juvenile literature. | Automobile racing--Juvenile literature. | Formula One automobiles--Juvenile literature. | Races (Sports)--Juvenile literature. | Encyclopedias and dictionaries--Juvenile literature.
Classification: DDC 796.72--dc23